CELTA CATS

ROBIN D. OWENS

COPYRIGHT

ISBN-10: 1981709207

ISBN-13: 978-1981709205

❀ Created with Vellum

CONTENTS

INTRODUCTION

I started writing FamCat's (intelligent cat Familiar Companion's) point of view stories for my blog and newsletter. After I got three, I thought I'd do several more for this collection.

Two of these stories tell about events that readers have requested (Zanth Gets His Boy, Pinky Becomes A Fam). A couple fill in events in the timeline that I wanted to show (Zanth Finds The Treasure, Baccat Claims His Fam). And the other two explore characters that readers want to know better: Zanth, the all-time favorite FamCat, and Peaches, the *first* FamCat we see, traveling through space on the starship *Nuada's Sword*.

The last section of this volume contains an *out take*. I tend to write long and cut scenes and stories. Usually this is because the scene has a lot of background and world building I don't actually need to show. This happened while writing the stories, too.

My newsletter readers will have seen three of these stories before, but three are completely new. The older ones were, in chronological order: Zanth Gets His Boy, Pinky Becomes A Fam, and Zanth Claims The Treasure. The new stories are: Peaches Arrives On Celta, and Baccat Chooses His Person, and Zanth Saves The Day.

None of these stories have previously been published in ebook or in print.

I hope you enjoy your journey to and time on Celta, and appreciate the FamCats...

PEACHES ARRIVES ON CELTA

*I introduced Peaches in the story **Heart And Sword**, a sexy romance that takes place on the starship, **Nuada's Sword** while it still journeyed to Celta (while it was lost). So, in the history of Celta Cats, he'd have been the first major Familiar Companion.*

Here he is again, in events that start a little after the main problem of Heart And Sword resolved, but showing the landing of Nuada's Sword on the planet that became Celta.

ON THE STARSHIP *Nuada's Sword,* 275 Years After Leaving Earth

Peaches, the smart Familiar Companion Cat, sat on a thin couch cushion in the dark, small lounge. He looked out a huge porthole that showed the planet which would be his new home. So did nine other Familiar companions who'd joined him. Four other Cats and five dogs.

He studied the darkness of *outer space* beyond the window, and the hanging sphere of the planet. Even the Fams had become accustomed to the notion of a planet as a new home, and could recognize the round ball floating in space as their target. They would live *outside the Ship* where they'd all been born and grown up. Scary idea. His fur ruffled at the thought.

He twitched a sore ear, still scabbed over from his last fight.

Last month, Peaches' FamMan, Randolph, had fallen in with bad people and joined a conspiracy. Randolph hadn't discovered how evil the group was until after they'd killed the former Captain and shot Grandmother Chloe.

Needless to say, Grandmother Chloe was having a hard time forgiving FamMan Randolph. But enough time had passed that she *should* forgive him. Lately she'd been mean.

But FamMan Randolph had lost face when his friends had been revealed to be bad guys, and Peaches' own status had plummeted. So he'd had to fight and do other stuff to regain status for both himself and his FamMan.

Peaches had managed to finagle the treat of a Fam-only viewing from the new Captain of the Ship. That had spared Peaches several more fights to prove himself, again, Top Cat and Top Fam.

He'd used his smarts instead of teeth and claws.

This time.

And *someone* continued to spread rumors about the Captain and FamMan, telling lies. One of the Fams had been telling lies about Peaches, too. So he continued to need to prove himself Top Fam, the Fam the others would listen to and follow.

They—*he*—had to find the bad person and stop him or her, both the human and Fam.

But who were they?

He sensed two more Cats and one puppy still doubted his primary rank. Didn't help that the unattached Fam puppy had her eye on the new Captain Lady of the starship,

Nuada's Sword. That woman had more prestige than Peaches' FamMan, Randolph Ash.

Status meant everything to Cats. Less for dogs, but all the Fams knew their place in the order of things. Smarter Cats like Peaches made better decisions than lower Fams who did not think as much and did not talk well with their humans or among the rest of the Fams.

Deep in his throat he grumbled to himself. He would not have had to prove his status again if his human hadn't been foolish. But his human, Randolph, had made bad friends. Those bad friends had done bad things without Randolph knowing, then got caught. And now lies about FamMan and Captain and Peaches were being believed.

Peaches clicked his tongue at the waste of time of it all. Everyone on all of the starship, *Nuada's Sword*, should just *know* Peaches was Top Fam, and a *good* Fam.

Randolph's grandmother also grumbled much, and out loud and with anger at FamMan.

And she fussed about the name FamMan should take. Peaches understood the importance of good names, and some Family names had been *reserved* for those who had paid for the trip. Grandmother had been one of those. She and Randolph had taken a name and now she doubted the wisdom of her choice. Because FamMan had smudged it or something.

Peaches also thought Grandmother, like many people, was afraid of going down to the planet and took out her fear on FamMan Randolph.

As he squashed his own fear into a tiny ball, he noticed the planet had *moved* and showed more land than ocean.

Pretty! the puppy burbled the words into all their minds. *Pretty blue and pretty green and pretty blue and green.*

puppies.

A Cat older than Peaches snorted. *Pretty means NOTH-ING. My FamWoman says we don't know enough about it. Other animals or even plants or dirt might hurt us.*

My FamMan says we aren't going to land safely, a dog said gloomily. *We will all die. Here or there.*

I think I will hide on my pillow under my blanket when we land, decided another dog.

All the Fams living on board the starship turned their heads to stare at Peaches. He understood the most about this landing-and-new-home business. His FamMan was smart—a genius—about science and the planet. Randolph *had* finally helped *good* people figure out how to get to a new home.

Captain and Captain Lady had sent *labs* and *probes* to check on planet. Labs had crashed, but the probes had come back. Smart scientist FamMan Randolph had studied and studied the dirt and revealed the world would be good to live on.

And Peaches knew the Captain and the Captain Lady, and the Pilot. All three who'd traveled in tubes in a special room and had to be Awakened to handle bad people, but that had finished *days* ago.

An air of gloom pervaded the small lounge, some negative feelings leftover from humans' sad emotions. Cats—Fams—were *sensitive* to that.

Peaches hated gloom. He pumped up his own optimism, said what needed to be said, truth or not. *Of course We will make it! My FamMan is the best and he helped a lot with the discovery! THIS IS AN ADVENTURE!*

doggy smiles with lolling tongues and drool.

Cat sniffs and snorts.

Peaches ignored the nasty twinge in his gut. He also knew, and wasn't talking, about how Pilot had kill-everybody buttons on the arm of her chair. If landing went really, really bad, or if the planet was poisonous, she could explode them all.

Such fear curled in his belly and would make him scared if he let it.

They *would* land. Yes.

And the planet would be like FamMan Randolph said. He reminded the Fams mentally, *MY FamMan says being on planet will be like being in Ship's Great Greensward Park.* They all loved playing in the park, sniffing the scents others left.

More happiness flowed from them, less sad and fear. Cheerful Cat and dog and puppy mutters sounded in his mind and ears.

"Fam viewing time in the small lounge is now over. Please leave the area," announced the Ship.

Time to remind Peaches' fellow Fams of *why* he was Top Fam. Because of his smarts. He addressed the also smart being who housed them, the intelligent starship, *Nuada's Sword. Ship, Landing will be fun, right?*

"An adventure," Ship agreed.

You have been on a planet before, too, right? Peaches pressed.

"Yes," Ship replied. A pause and all ears cocked. "I have fulfilled my purpose. I am looking forward to not traveling and being responsible for all the lives of my friends. I would like a new and solid home to sit on."

Peaches hadn't heard that before. He would tell his FamMan and the Captain and the Captain Lady.

Outside is like the Great Greensward! Peaches emphasized for the less smart Fams.

"So we believe," Ship said, talking about the top people, including Peaches. Ship opened the doors that slid into the walls.

Sighs from the Cats and dogs as they hopped down from the porthole ledge and filed out the door. On the whole, they radiated satisfaction.

Peaches had fixed some of the negativity.

And he'd watched the other Fams so he would figure out who might be lying about him, so he could fix that.

He'd have to fix grandmother, too, so she wouldn't be scared and wouldn't continue to hurt FamMan's feelings. And maybe *break* their little family of three.

He sent one last glance at the pretty planet and wondered with sweaty pads whether they would really get there.

THE FAMS MOVED into the bright corridor and mixed around as a group. Very rarely did they gather together in the huge Ship. Now they murmured together in Cat or dog, and in mental mumbles along their shared stream. They enjoyed their own furry company, not just being with their FamPerson and a bunch of other humans.

The hallway looked different than a while ago. When the new Captain had come Awake from his tube, he began fixing things and making people happier. Peaches approved. And when Ship woke up Captain Lady, she filled the Captain with joy.

Peaches ticked off the days on his claws, more than *eighteen days* had passed since that happened. If the time was longer than four paws of claws, he ignored it. Humans cared too much about time. All good now.

Still, he sniffed in approval at the pleasant scent of the pretty flowers in the new boxes along the wall. The tint of the wall looked different to his cat eyes, seemed to please human eyes more.

He flexed his claws, the non-skid floor felt cleaner on his pads than since he'd been a kitten.

"Whatcha see in the viewing lounge, Fams? Huh, think of that, a private viewing session for *Fams!*" a man jeered.

The stupid man's own FamCat, black-and-gray Stripey, hissed at him.

The guy sneered down at Peaches. "You're afraid, aren't you? Of burning up in a fireball when landing, or a poisonous planet?" Man said scary stuff no one wanted to hear. Old fear sweat seemed to coat his whole body, caught in his clothes, lingering on the centuries-old recycled Ship air.

I'm not afraid! Peaches said, a little uneasily. To prove it, even to himself, Peaches put his tail up—too many Fams walking with their tails down—and waved it back and forth. Again, he stated, *loudly* this time for the stupider humans in the corridor, *The planet will be like the Great Greensward park!*

Me love park! rumbled an younger dog, also waving his tail, too thick and plumey for Peaches' preference. *Me love park best except FamMan's bed.*

Stripey grumbled under his breath, but went over to strop his cranky FamMan's ankles.

PEACHES IS RIGHT! I LIKE PEACHES, loudly projected the oldest dog, the one with much white on his muzzle. He moved slowly, but had smarts and hadn't ever challenged Peaches, so Peaches liked him the best of all the Fams.

Peaches is a stupid name, Stripey said.

Peaches narrowed his eyes and looked at the Cat who'd never said anything to him before about his name. A challenge.

And now he sensed Stripey had been the one telling lies about him.

Stripey. Of course it had to be Stripey. Stripey, older than Peaches, who wanted to be Top Fam. He and Peaches had fought before.

Stripey had let his lying FamMan influence him poorly, instead of Stripey persuading his FamMan to make better decisions. That showed a lack of character on both their parts.

Stripey and his FamMan must be stopped from telling lies.

Peaches would deal with Stripey first. *STRIPE-EY,* he sneered back. *Ey-names are for young ones. My FamMan is RANDOLPH. Only Rand-Y when boy.* He paused, deciding whether to add another insult when the man picked up his Fam and Stripey purred.

"Stupid *Peaches.* Stupid name, stupid cat," the man said.

Peaches hunkered down and flattened his ears. *Yes, this man had influenced Stripey!*

Peaches didn't care much for his name based on his coloring, but no one should mock him for it. He'd gotten it as an adorable kitten, of course. He remained completely adorable, but it didn't quite fit the tough and dominant Top Fam he'd become.

He stared at the man with mean creases in his pudgy face. The guy had fat face and round little belly and stick arms and legs. Not as good looking a human as Peaches was Cat. One of the reasons Peaches was Top Fam was because of his looks. Fine legs and back, athletic torso, beautiful whiskers, beautiful orange and white fur, adorable cream tufted ears.

Peaches lifted his nose, trod over to the man, whisked around and lifted his tail as if to spray.

The man yelped and hopped back and fell off balance

and dropped Stripey. Who had to twist to land on his feet and hissed disapproval.

Pity you for that FamMan, Peaches said privately to Stripey. *I remember his sire, a much better and nicer man. One who liked Cats.* Peaches sniffed at Stripey. *Pity you.*

Then Peaches made his mental voice loud enough for all Fams and humans to hear in their heads and said, *Be glad you didn't learn that I don't smell like peaches.* Other people laughed and Peaches sauntered down the corridor, tail up, white tip waving.

Without looking, he sent last words back so now all Fams could hear. *We will settle this later, Stripey.*

"Hey, Peaches, there you are!" Randolph FamMan turned into the corridor and hurried down it. Peaches put on some speed and shot toward him. Randolph opened his arms and Peaches leapt into them. FamMan caught him and laughed. Peaches' purr filled the hall along with a couple of human chuckles.

FamMan said a magic-spell Word to use his psi power magic, Flair, and made a spell to keep Peaches easily on his shoulder. Felt like an invisible, solid shelf big enough for Peaches' backside.

Randolph, too, was skinny, not growing into his full form yet since humans considered him just turned into an adult at eighteen years.

Well, most humans. Randolph's Father's Mother, Grandma Chloe, now nagged and picked at and scolded like he'd dropped back to boyhood for his foolish mistakes.

"Stupid Fams," snapped Stripey's man, red in the face. His lip curled. "And there's Peaches' equally stupid human owner."

Peaches growled, no one owned him.

Randolph stiffened under Peaches. "Foolish I may be,

but not stupid. I chose my friends poorly, against my Fam's and my Grandmother's advice. I'm *not* stupid enough to call Fams names." He reached up and scratched Peaches between his ears. "You should know better than to insult Fams, Lewis-Y Munz." Randolph inclined his head, then turned on his heel and walked away.

Well done, Peaches complimented His human.

Randolph's mouth quirked up. *I'm learning.*

STUPID PEACHES! yelled Stripey along the Fam only mental stream. *We will settle this. I will be top cat. I am oldest.*

Yesss, Peaches agreed, turning his head and angling it down to Stripey who stood on the floor. *We will hash this out. I am the Best.* Then Peaches looked ahead, not having to hide his smirk. He knew more about Stripey than Stripey knew about him, and Peaches would use his smarts to beat him.

❧

A FEW HALLS away they stopped at the door near the Captain's quarters where Randolph's Grandma Chloe lived.

The door slid open to reveal a small room with built-in metal furniture to sleep on, sit on, and store stuff.

"You're late," Chloe snapped, her old face crinkling into the pattern of the many lines. She stood, hands on hips, tapping her foot.

Her skin showed one tint darker than most humans. "We're expected in Conference Room A in five minutes to meet with the newly *Awakened* colonists." She touched her white hair, stopped before she ran her fingers through it like she often did.

"Time enough," Randolph soothed.

Peaches thought so. The thin woman walked slower

now, but even dawdling they should get there by the time a paw's worth of minutes had passed.

"We must leave." Peaches heard her teeth click together. Not a good sign.

"Grandmother—*Grandma*—"   Randolph   spurted forward to the old woman and Peaches had to whisk his tail around him before the door closed.

Her face scrunched in deep lines and Peaches gut tightened. "Randy," she snipped back.

FamMan heard the tone, too. His face went blank but he continued walking up to her and put his arms around her. Peaches noticed a while back that Grandma Chloe had shrunk since he was a kitten. He recalled her much bigger. But she carried great responsibility. She was high up in Ship status, *The Executive Officer.* Second to the Captain, and she helped run the Ship.

That burdensome duty, and the death of the previous Captain, had worn on her.

Right now, everyone except Grandma and the Captain and Captain Lady and the pilot had been born on the Ship, for many generations.

And those people who Grandma Chloe and the Captain Lady had *Awakened* from the tubes today. Might have been tiring, maybe that's why she grouched.

"You used to call me Randolph," he murmured, rocking with her in comfort.

Peaches leaned down from his perch on FamMan's shoulder and and purred near her head.

She moved a little in his arms, looked up at him, panted out words, "Before your friends *shot* me!" She stepped away and put her hand over her side.

FamMan closed his eyes and wavered a little on his feet.

Peaches decided he wanted to be on his feet, too. So he jumped down.

Before FamMan could apologize again, Peaches reminded her, *FAMMAN SAVED YOU!*

He shouted from his mind to theirs. *FAMMAN SAVED ALL OF US! We are going to LIVE on a planet. YOU remember living on a planet, don't you?* He sat on his rump near her toes and looked up and gave her the big cheerful eyes and quivering-with-joy whiskers.

Her mouth opened, but this time only a shaky breath went into her. She glanced down at him, then her eyes seemed to blur as if she looked into a-long-time-ago.

You can help us! Peaches enthused. Grandma Chloe liked being helpful best. *Because you know about living Outside.*

"Yes." The word quavered. Her lips pursed then flattened. When she spoke, she sounded stronger. "Outside can be beautiful...."

We will make it so! Peaches revved his purr, ignoring his own doubts.

Her shoulders relaxed and when she bent down and petted him, she moved less stiff with fear.

"Yes, the planet Celta will be beautiful and we will make it a home."

Thanks to FamMan Randolph! Peaches backed the words with a mind purr.

Grandma Chloe straightened. "Yes, Randolph—"

Helped A LOT.

"Yes," she sighed and touched the badge on her shirt as if reassuring herself of her status as Executive Officer, motioned at the door and it slid open behind Randolph. "Let's go confer with the newly Awakened." She fingered her badge again. "Everyone is expecting us."

FamMan ran his hand along her arm in support. "I

redeemed myself by helping the Captain put down the conspiracy and working hard on determining that this planet has the physical characteristics to become a good home. Grandmother, you, as always, are doing an excellent job."

"Yes." Out she walked, head high and with purpose.

Randolph sighed, too, and scooped Peaches up. Over their private mental line, Randolph said, *Thank you, Peaches. She is good for now, but she's not done with complaining. I believe she fears landing. Perhaps she believes she is too old to found a new world and family and thrive.*

Shock reverberated through Peaches. He hadn't thought of that. *We must make her feel better.*

You're doing well, too, Randolph said.

Peaches increased his purr. *We both are.*

But FamMan's lips turned down, like he knew their problems weren't over. And Peaches' gut squeezed at the thought of the big, black space outside and the planet far away.

DURING THE MEETING in the luxurious conference room, a whiny woman fussing about names and pretending to be allergic to Peaches dominated the time. The seven other colonists who'd slept in the tubes and been *Awakened* just watched and listened.

Peaches didn't care too much about the tube people. He and FamMan had been born on the Ship. He and FamMan cared more about the crew people like them than the people who bought the Ship and paid for the trip.

Grandma Chloe grumbled to the other colonists about the name she'd picked and FamMan Randolph had taken.

She implied he hadn't lived up to the good name, riling Peaches and depressing the spirits of Randolph.

Just as Peaches thought of protesting, Grandma Chloe made the entire window wall open to outer space for some of the colonists, disturbing Peaches with the huge black and pinpoint colorful stars and the looming planet.

Finally, Chloe said to FamMan Randolph, "Randy, why don't you lead our friends on a tour of the GreatGreensward."

She spoke to him like he hadn't become an adult the last month, more, like he hadn't reached his tenth Nameday.

With a brief nod to Grandma Chloe, Randolph kept the doors open as everyone filed out, Captain Lady first, patting Randolph on the shoulder.

Grandma Chloe and Peaches remained after the doors of the conference room closed. She tidied up the leftover drink tubes and discarded scraps of papyrus with lists of names. When she made the portal a wall again, Peaches jumped onto the big, fancy wood table and stared at her, keeping his whiskers stiff, radiating disapproval to Grandma.

She scowled at him. "What?"

YOU disappoint ME!

She flinched.

FamMan is good. He is respected by good people, by the Captain and Captain Lady. You should not show you might doubt him in front of others. And you should not doubt him!

Grandma Chloe stiffened herself. *I have a right to my feelings.*

Peaches stopped himself from accusing her of being afraid. He gentled his mind tone. *Yes, but you should not take away the name you chose for yourself, the surname you gave FamMan Randolph years ago.*

She swallowed hard. "I *do* have doubts."

Do you not also have faith? Faith in how you raised FamMan? Faith that he is a good man? Did he not SHOW EVERYONE that he is good by redeeming himself?

Grandma Chloe reached out and gripped the solid edge of the wood table, lowered herself into the cloth cushioned metal chair. Like everyone else who'd been in the conference room, she stroked the wood. Not much wood in the Ship outside of the GreatGreensward, where trees lived. Very valuable.

And this expensive table had been crafted on Earth, itself.

You should at least tell Randolph that you will keep the name ASH, like he has.

Chloe sniffed and her eyes looked big with water.

"I don't—"

I will remind you that he is all the family you have left.

She flinched.

Hurting him will make him not want to be with you.

She hunched over.

Instead of just feeling, THINK! And have faith in him and in US all. Peaches leapt from the table and sauntered to the doors that opened for him.

He'd told her what she should do. Now she should follow his advice. His own feelings should follow his head, too.

❧

EARLY THE NEXT MORNING, Peaches slipped away from their quarters through his favorite air duct, leaving his humans to sleep while he took care of Stripey.

Grandma Chloe had only been a little mean at dinner

because she'd been tired from *Awakening* a few more tube-people.

Peaches thought that his disapproval of her also made her *think*.

She hadn't told FamMan Randolph that they would continue to carry the name 'Ash,' so Peaches hadn't quite fixed that problem like he'd thought he had.

But he'd fix the one with lying Stripey, and rise to the status of Top Fam on the Ship once more. Then he'd figure out how to deal with Stripey's lying man.

Fams and his status among them was more important right now. He had to keep them thinking positive about the landing and the new world, so they would keep their humans from gloom and despair.

He knew his target. Stripey liked to pee in the Great-Greensward when daylight-time began. He would get a surprise!

He'd get a challenge by Peaches.

Peaches had already sent a low level "come" spell out to the other Fams so they could see the fight and watch him triumph. Might even stop the last Cat from challenging him.

Sometimes you couldn't talk, you had to fight.

He slid down a tube into the GreatGreensward close to the area Stripey liked best and marked most. Staying off the gravel paths humans preferred, Peaches stalked through the short, thick grass near low bushes, noting that other Fams hid nearby.

He spotted Stripey and swaggered close behind him.

Stripey squatted.

Greetyou, STRIPEY!

Stripey leapt up, turned in mid-air, landed, scowling at Peaches, hissed. *This MY territory. MY time.*

Peaches rolled a shrug. *Thought We should talk.*

Stripey lifted the top of his muzzle in a fanged sneer. *You YAMMER too much.*

That stung.

And you don't talk well, Stripey sneered. Flattening his ears, Stripey began his growl, sounding all through the range of Cat hearing.

Peaches responded with his lower growl, heard other Fams shift around until they circled Stripey and him.

Narrowing his eyes, he waited. The first to attack meant he lacked control, would lose face. Peaches would have to be fast to retaliate.

Stripey launched himself on Peaches, who moved, rolled, twisted. Stripey only got a swipe on his side. Hurt!

They rolled. He put his feet up, protecting his belly, digging into Stripey's soft stomach flesh. Peaches felt a bite near his neck, bit Stripey on his ear, ripped it *good*. Felt more blood trickle from a puncture on his own side. Another twist, flip, *strike* had Stripey submitting.

Panting. Bleeding.

Are you done, now, StripEY? he spit the phrase along a mental channel.

Done, Peaches. You are Top Cat. Top Fam. And I am not Stripey no more. I'm STRIPED, now. Call Me Striped.

Peaches hopped back.

You will spread no more lies about Me? he demanded.

No, Peaches.

He stared at his opponent. Looked like Striped lost a fight. Peaches tested his own muscles. He carried wounds that would have to heal.

Okay, Striped, he addressed the Cat.

Youngest Cat trotted up, ducked her head, gave a small, rumbling purr. *You are Top Cat, Peaches.* She paused, glanced around her. *Top Fam. Me didn't believe no lies about You,* she added virtuously.

None of the other dogs or Cats protested.

Good! Peaches flicked his tail, suppressed a yowl. Striped had gotten in a good claw on his tail, too, but his fur would hide wound until FamMan Randolph or Grandma Chloe could put medicine on his hurts.

With an eye on Peaches, Striped rolled to his feet, limped away.

Peaches followed him to a different tube than he used before, to watch him and his FamMan. This tube would whisk them to a corridor far above the GreatGreensward into the main public areas of the crew. Fine with him. Everyone would see he'd won back his title of Top Fam.

The other Fams stayed in the huge park area, cheered that all status was back to normal, maybe talking about the short battle. Youngest Cat got distracted by hunting mice.

One problem, easiest, taken care of. Now to see how he could stop Striped's FamMan, Lewisy, from lying about Peaches' FamMan.

As soon as Peaches slid out of the tube into a near empty corridor, a man yelled, *"You hurt my cat!"* Striped's mean-voiced-FamMan, Lewisy, yelled.

Long bony fingers attached to a sweaty hand grabbed Peaches by the scruff of his neck! He squealed...and didn't stop the sound from going to FamMan Randolph. Who woke and *teleported* into the hallway in his pajamas.

People gasped. Not many could move from one place to another in an instant.

The fingers dropped Peaches and FamMan grabbed him, put him on his shoulder.

Peaches hissed at Striped's FamMan. Striped huddled close by the wall, embarrassed that his defeat showed to everybody in his half-torn ear. Mortified that his FamMan arrived too late to any call Striped had made. And now his FamMan, Lewisy, mixed in Fam Business. Humiliating for Striped.

Peaches sent his senses throughout the area, *felt* the Captain in a nearby training room. So he said telepathically to Randolph, *Move back two doors.* If this disturbance grew, the Captain would sense it and come out.

What? Randolph asked, but followed Peaches' advice, fading back a few meters.

"You there!" Mean-man pointed a finger at FamMan. "Randolph...Ash?"

FamMan's shoulder stiffened under Peaches' rump. Gossip must have spread through the Ship that Grandma Chloe doubted keeping the Ash name because of Randolph's old actions of last month.

Peaches hissed at the guy, but FamMan answered nice, "Yes, GentleSir Munz?"

"The Captain co-opted you," Lewisy sneered. "You abandoned the reg'lar people for the *sleepers*, the elite." He hitched up his belt over his little belly, waved passersby to stop and listen. Some did.

Randolph replied, "Because the Captain and my Grandmother were right! We can't live on the Ship forever, travel forever. We were running out of fuel, the planet we're heading for is our best chance. Best for the other starships, *Lugh's Spear* and *Arianrhod's Wheel,* too, who are also in dire straits."

"Don' care about them," Munz said.

"Obviously not," said Grandma Chloe, hurrying into view.

"And *you* have always been with the elite!"

She stood next to FamMan and Peaches, smaller so Peaches could have stepped down onto her lower shoulder. But she would have to use psychic magic power, *Flair*, to hold him.

"Of course," Grandma Chloe said. "On Earth I lived and fought in the ghetto for psi people. Fought against mobs who called everyone who used Flair 'mutant.' Neither the government nor the people liked those of us who were different.

"I bought shares in this enterprise that purchased the starships and supplies and hired the crew." She looked at the other humans. "I believed, and still believe, in a better future *for us all, especially those gifted with psi.*"

"Which is pretty much all of us," Randolph said, "including you, Lewisy. I can sense your Flair."

Moderate, Peaches sent to FamMan and Grandma Chloe.

In her hand she held the thing that showed squiggles and pictures. Nothing interesting. Glancing down, she said, "GentleSir Lewisy Munz. You're a supply officer." She glanced up at him and though her expression looked calm, Peaches felt anger emanating from her. FamMan went still. "A rather high status job. Are you worried about your future on the planet as opposed to here?"

"You gave away some of my supplies. Two tons of meal bars!"

Her hand went to her side, and came up with a bar, she'd *translocated* from somewhere else. "Yes, the starship *Lugh's Spear* needed the food and the subsistence sticks. We sent them to them."

"Lies! You wanted them for yourselves and you *sold* them to *Lugh's Spear.*"

You are the one who lies. And you do not listen! Peaches put in.

"No, neither the Captain nor I lied." Grandma stated. "The facts are clear. You can check them. And we sent the food four weeks ago. You're still whining about that? Did you *eat* one of those sticks?"

Again she looked around. "Did anyone here?"

"I tasted one. Terrible." A young woman stuck out her tongue.

"So the Captain and my Grandma didn't lie about that, did they?" Randolph smiled. "How many more meal sticks do we have, Executive Officer Chloe Ash? We can afford to give GentleSir Munoz hundreds, can't we? See if he can sell them to whomever."

"Oh, yes." Grandma Chloe bobbed her head. "We can fill up your bunk with crates."

Someone snickered.

Face turning red, Striped's man shifted from one little human foot to another. Big ego, moderate Flair, puny smarts. "Maybe you never sent the bars, that's why you still have a lot of them." His lips twisted and he jerked his chin up, revealing a scrawny neck. "Lies. The elite only want to keep us down, everything they say are lies," he stated. As a crowd gathered, his skinny frame puffed up in importance. "And they're lying to us, making fake projections on our portholes. There really is *no* planet."

Striped sat up, lifted a paw, licked it, and touched his bleeding ear. *Always knew round ball in window was fake. Looks fake. Nothing like that is real. No planet, only Ship.*

Peaches hissed down at his former opponent.

Striped shifted uneasily, winced as if movement hurt. *Didn't mean to challenge you again, Peaches. They fool you, too!*

YOU HAVE AS LITTLE SMARTS AS THAT MAN. *MY* FAMMAN HAS LOTS OF SMARTS, LIKE ME! All is real! I will show you the Landing Bay, Striped! Peaches snapped. He would not let lies stand, let himself be called a fool. The words would lead to a dip in his status. *You can feel the cold of space outside.* He jumped from FamMan Randolph's shoulder and lit lightly.

Striped pressed back against the wall, good.

Peaches glanced up at Lewisy with a grin. *You will let him stay in the bay and let us open the door so you can see that he can't breathe—*

"No!" shouted FamMan and grandmother Chloe.

Peaches swaggered to Striped, within good sniffing range. Striped smelled of fear. Peaches lifted his nose. *Of course to keep you safe you will need to be stuffed in a nasty suit.* He looked up at the mean man. *But you don't care about that, either, do you? You don't care about your FamCat.*

The door opened near FamMan Randolph and the Captain stepped from the room, looking more dangerous than anyone Peaches had ever seen.

"You think we lie to you? Is that so?" the Captain asked smoothly. With a gesture, other tough guys, *security guards,* gathered around him, and everyone faded back to give them room.

Peaches stood and waved his tail, shouted so all the dim humans could hear his mental words. *I WILL TAKE STRIPED TO LANDING BAY. HE CAN BE IN A SUIT. WE WILL OPEN THE *DOOR* TO THE SHIP AND HE CAN SEE OUTER SPACE AND THE PLANET HIMSELF!*

People gasped, but everyone looked interested.

Striped's claws scrabbled on thin non-stick floor panels, the metal walls, trying to get purchase. *Nooo!* he wailed.

The Captain cleared his throat. "I will not be a party to the endangerment of an animal..."

Peaches glared at him.

"Or a Familiar Companion."

He nodded to Lewisy, swept a hand around to those gathered. "Come, if you need proof of what we say, that we have found a new world to live on."

"You lie! You lie all the time! This is nothing but a big lie!" Peaches actually saw little bits of spit dry near the ends of Lewisy's mouth.

"Then we'll fit *you* with a spacesuit, open the bay and let you go out on a tether. You can tell us whether there's a planet floating in space or not," Grandma Chloe said sweetly.

And you can see whether this is all true or not, Peaches said. *We will ALL watch. People who believe like you do!* He swiveled his neck around to people who had been smirking at him, at the Captain, doing the thumbs-up thing to stupid, mean man.

"I can help him into the spacesuit, monitor his vital signs," FamMan Randolph said. He swung on his heel and stared at the disbelievers. "There's an observation room next to Landing Bay. It should accommodate all of you who'd like to watch Lewisy's excursion."

The Captain grinned, rocked lightly on his feet. "Yep, you can be just a hardglass window away from outer space. See outside yourselves."

Now some of those people looked scared.

"A good way to verify those facts you doubt," said FamMan Randolph. "*In person.*"

Human pride not as touchy as Cat pride, but these

people would lose face if they did not go. And Lewisy would be shown to be deeply stupid if he did not accept the challenge. Well, he was deeply stupid and would be shown that either way, but he'd also be shown to be *wrong*. That the lies *he* had spewed *were lies.*

Peaches and FamMan Randolph and Captain and Captain Lady and Pilot told the truth. Wanted best for *everyone.* FamMan's old bad friends, like this Lewisy, had only wanted best for themselves.

Peaches looked for Striped. He'd vanished down the hallway, maybe hiding behind a couple of bigger dogs a few meters away.

Come on, Striped! Peaches sent through the Familiar Companion mental stream to all the Fams.

No, thank you, Top Fam Peaches, I believe you now!

A dog rumbled, *Fams smarter than some humans.*

The Captain said, "We need a good test of the opening of the human landing bay door anyway." He rolled heavy shoulders, nodded to FamMan Randolph. "First Science Officer, please proceed."

Randolph appeared slightly stunned.

Captain nodded at him, "We had a consultation and decided that since you've been doing the job of a First Science Officer, you should hold the title."

"Thank you," murmured Randolph. Then he sucked in breath and swept a hand around the group, "GentleSirs, GentleLadies, follow me." Then he stepped close and put his wide hand around Lewisy's biceps. "Come along. We'll get this matter straightened out." He smiled big. "And if you want a few hundred subsistence sticks, we can give those to you, too."

"Yessss," Peaches vocalized, strolling behind marching FamMan and shuffling Lewisy.

Mean man was *stuck*.

Grandma Chloe joined them, still fiddling with her flat mechanical thing. "I've decided we were right in keeping the name, 'Ash.' We're Ashes."

Her words were nice, Peaches had done some fixing there, but he and FamMan shared a serious glance. Grandma had only grudgingly accepted something she'd tried to take away, the name that had been set long ago. A last name she'd chosen and given to Randolph as a baby.

Randolph's lips turned up again and said telepathically to Peaches. *We're Ashes again.*

We always have been, Peaches grumbled.

We managed to smooth that disagreement over, but she still fears the future. We must do better. *I* must do better.

SHE must do better, Peaches replied.

FAMMAN STOOD at the glassed in console in Landing Bay. Peaches admired his courage, but sat in the observation room next door on a cabinet next to the floor-to-ceiling window. Some of the people in the corridor hadn't made it to the observation room. They'd faded away due to fear. Only ten or so humans came to watch, and only three Fams, including Peaches. Striped had returned to his quarters.

Just beside Peaches' cabinet, an older, mid-sized dog leaned against the glass wall. Peaches had touched the wall and found it cool. He knew when the Landing Bay doors to *outer space* opened, the glass would turn frigid. He shivered a little and hoped with all his heart that FamMan remained safe in the cubicle. For an instant, he wished he were back on FamMan's bed and not having to look out into darkness with stars and planet again.

Lewisy clumsily got into the space suit that went over his clothes. At least he would have arms and legs free. If Striped had been stupid and prideful enough to do this, he would have been in more of a bubble, with no control of his limbs in relation to the outside environment.

The Captain put a helmet on Lewisy and made sure it attached good. Captain patted all of the openings to the suit, checking them. Peaches got the idea Captain felt fiercely amused.

Captain attached a flexible metal cable to Lewisy's belt. The other end of the cable came from inside the wall of the Ship. Peaches figured that end was really, really safe, but didn't know about Lewisy's belt. Peaches was glad he hadn't been stupid or prideful enough to do this, either. A person should always watch his words that might lead to devastating challenges.

Taking Lewisy's arm, the Captain walked him to the edge of the door. "You'll be fine," Captain said.

"Wait." FamMan Randolph exited the small cubicle and crossed to the two men. His lips moved as he murmured Words, magic spell words, and the suit glowed. "Added Flair shields we've developed against the vacuum of outer space," Randolph said. He smiled with white teeth. "Should do great, though we haven't tested them, yet." He returned to the glass case.

The Captain tapped his fingers on Lewisy's helmet and making pinging sounds, and said, "Later," to Lewisy, turned his back on the now trembling man — Peaches thought the suit looked to be for a larger guy than Lewisy — and sauntered from the room. Now only FamMan Randolph, in his glass cube, and Lewisy in a space suit, remained in the huge Landing Bay.

"Let's check the communication out," FamMan

Randolph said. He flicked a few switches, and Peaches realized the quick whooshes he heard and the rapid thump-thump-thump, came from Lewisy's lungs and heart. Scared. Ha!

"Your vitals statistics read a little high," FamMan said. "Let's test the communication now. Can you hear me?"

"Yes," replied Lewisy. It sounded tinny.

"Try again," Randolph said.

"YES!" This time the word boomed throughout the Landing Bay, and the observation room, and Peaches even heard it in the corridor.

"I've initiated Ship-wide cameras and audio for this first Space Walk," FamMan said

"Space walk?" Lewisy squeaked.

"Opening the Landing Bay doors," Randolph said. His hands moved over the console.

"No!" Lewisy cried, too late.

The huge inner rectangular doors split horizontally and disappeared into the floor and the ceiling with metal grumblings.

"No," Lewisy whimpered, turning his back away from the door.

"Iris door opening is initiated," FamMan said. The eye-iris shaped door slowly opened in a circular motion.

Gasps echoed throughout the Ship from everyone watching. Peaches wasn't ashamed to admit he gasped, too. Maybe shrank a little against the nice, solid wall.

"Landing Bay Earthan atmosphere depleting, equalizing to zero grav and zero atmosphere matching the vacuum of space outside," Randolph said.

The dog jerked back from the glass, but watched. Everybody in the whole Ship watched, Peaches figured.

The world looked like it could almost float *inside*, bigger and more beautiful than seen through porthole windows. The star colors appeared a little different, too. Peaches' mouth dried.

And the planet seemed to move faster, he saw a brown-green land pattern he hadn't before.

"Zow," breathed FamMan Randolph. "What a view!"

"*What? No. What? No! What...NO!*" repeated Lewisy, his voice high and irritating.

"That, my friend, is space, and our new home, the world we've named Celta." Yearning laced Randolph's quiet tones. He cleared his throat, then said, "Just take a few steps outside of the Ship—"

A long, low wail came from the speakers as Lewisy flailed around. "*NO!*" He grabbed the edge of an outer wall and held on tightly. "*Don't make me go out there. No, no, no! Let me stay in!*"

FamMan hesitated, then said calmly, "You must release the edge of the wall, so I can close the doors."

"*I'll die, I'll die. There's nothing out there, outside of our Ship. It IS a starship and we're in the STARS.*"

"Exactly so," said Randolph. "Let go of the wall and I'll yank you back in to the safety of the Ship."

Lewisy shivered for a good minute more, then propelled himself back a little, then FamMan hit a button and the tether tied to his belt reeled in. Slowly the iris door closed, then the bigger ones snapped shut with a huge clunk.

Peaches found himself panting.

Landing Bay filled with good, breathable air quicker than Peaches had imagined. Before he thought about strolling in to meet his FamMan, the hall door opened and the Captain walked into the bay.

Lewisy saw him and waved his arms, jumped up and down once before collapsing.

"Let me out of this suit, let me out, *please!*"

"You sure we aren't lying to you, Lewisy Munz?" questioned the Captain softly, but with a dangerous edge to his voice.

Never wise call this Captain a liar, the oldest dog said. He shook his head like a human might. *Shoulda learned that lesson days and days ago.*

Peaches agreed.

"No, you don't lie! I've SEEN space. I experienced it. Now let me out of this suit!" Lewisy nearly wept.

Captain went over to Lewisy and squatted, began taking off his helmet. Captain's nose wrinkled. "Your bowels let loose in the suit, didn't they? Good thing it's self-cleansing."

At that moment, the door to the Ship opened and a tall woman with near white hair and curves humans prized strode in. She wore a spacesuit, too, and moved like it was as comfortable as regular clothes. She carried her helmet.

Her glance swept over FamMan Randolph and the Captain. "Wait!" she commanded.

The Captain rocked back on his heels. "Yes?"

"What's this about a space walk? Don't you think I should have been consulted? Since I am the only one who's ever actually been in space?"

"Uh," started the Captain.

"Events moved a little too quickly," FamMan Randolph said.

Pilot stopped at Lewisy, she showed no emotion at what must have been bad smells. "You want to try again, Lewisy? I'll be glad to accompany you. We can head out and check this area of the Ship's skin together."

"No," Lewisy said weakly, pushing his helmet off his head. "No, thank you."

With a jerk of a nod, she indicated to the Captain that

he should help Lewisy rise. Instead, the Captain hauled him up more roughly than Peaches would care to be treated. But the Captain had lots of muscles and Lewisy looked puny.

Pilot went to work and had Lewisy out of his suit in a few seconds. She was a professional, and, Peaches realized, as everyone else in the Ship did at the same time, *she* knew what to do. How to land Ship. And, of course, Ship had landed itself before.

They—the crew and the tube people colonists—could trust Pilot and Ship. A big sigh of relief came through Ship's speakers from many people.

Pilot put Lewisy's spacesuit carefully in the cleanser pod and activated it, dusted her hands and nodded to Captain and Randolph. "Any more need for me here? Or can I go back to consulting with Ship on orbital mechanics and the landing approach?"

Captain inclined his head. "Glad to have you here."

Pilot swept a glance around with a smile. "Glad to be here on this generational starship. Better than rotting in a ghetto or prison for psychically talented people on Earth. Of course, if they'd captured me before we took off, I'd've been long dead by now. Later, Captain. Later, First Science Officer. And, Randolph Ash, I need to pick your brain in the next day or two."

FamMan gulped, his voice came higher. "At your service, Pilot Larson."

She flashed him a smile. "Holly. I chose the surname of Holly for my new life."

FamMan bobbed his head.

She strode out. If she'd been a cat, her tail would have been twitching in satisfaction at showing her superior space suit skills.

Silence hung in the room as Peaches and the others watched Lewisy totter from the Landing Bay.

Randolph shoved a lever. "Initiating cameras outside Landing Bay and showing projections on the doors."

Once again dark space and bright stars and the big moving planet showed. This time not in real life through open doors.

Very interesting, said the old dog.

Peaches closed his eyes.

I hear they have bubbles for Fams, the puppy said. *I would like to go out and float in a bubble in space.*

Really stupid puppy.

"That's that. Disperse people," Grandma Chloe said. "Get back to work. And there will be plenty of work for *everyone* on Celta." She studied the gathering, looked down at her tablet of squiggles. "I see that most of you here have indicated the careers you want to follow down on Ea— Celta. Lewisy has been deleterious in doing that. He has no job or career. I suggest that those of you who haven't decided make up your mind soon." She shivered a little. "I have a hunch we will need every hand we can get to build Druida City and thrive on Celta."

I will help! Peaches offered, turning his back on space. They would get to Celta. Probably. *Fams can help!*

"Absolutely. I know your, and my grandson's, First Science Officer Randolph Ash's, capabilities."

Old dog walked out, *I can help, too. I can dig. I can smell good places for houses.*

I'll help! puppy bounced after him.

Later, Peaches and the rest of the Fams trotted through the trip, found out that Lewisy had been one of the last to say bad things about the Captain, to doubt the mission. And all grumblings had been laid to rest.

All focus was on the now, today, as it should be.

And the landing.

Some humans yet had a feeling of doom about getting from space to the world and solid ground itself.

For an instant Peaches stomach lurched. Ship had always felt like solid ground under his paws.

But, all in all, it had been a good day for Randolph and Peaches. Not one whisper of Randolph's past faults circulated in the gossip now. No, he was, as Peaches had considered him for a month, a hero. Doing the right thing in breaking away from the conspirators and those who thought of only living on the Ship, not going to a new world to live like humans and Fams should.

Even Grandma Chloe had mellowed. She'd taken them to the exclusive lounge dining room for the tube people and let them have the best food Peaches had tasted in his life. She'd rubbed Peaches' head and kissed FamMan Randolph on the cheek.

Peaches figured all would be well.

Until they actually began to land.

٭

A WEEK PASSED and humans kept busy. FamMan Randolph walked straighter and had special shirts that looked like Captain's and Captain Lady's and Grandma Chloe's and Pilot's and security guys' and a few others'. He pointed to a patch on a shirt and told Peaches it said, "First Science Officer."

He smiled all the time, enthusiastically answered questions by the crew about their new world and what plants and animals and other stuff they might find there. Apparently a long, long, *long* time ago, peoples who made Earth also made Celta. Peaches didn't understand that and it didn't bother him that he didn't understand it, but the knowledge made the humans happy.

Peaches asked the Fams to meet with him in a portion of the GreatGreensward full of flowers just before the landing. He was the only Fam to be descending to Celta in the Main Bridge. All around him would be humans, and he wanted some last moments with beings like himself.

And he confirmed his status as Top Fam when all gathered when he asked them.

They all radiated fear or terror and Peaches kept his own anxiety locked away from the others. Did not leak it. Kept his calm.

They had merged into a more cohesive unit than had ever happened in their generations aboard the Ship. They remembered their purpose, to help their human Familiar Companions, and other people. To comfort. To advise.

The flowers and dirt reminded them all where they were going, what they were giving up life on Ship for, huge new territory for them all, dirt and plants and playtime in something like a Greensward whenever they wanted.

Fabulous smells.

At Peaches' prompting, they agreed to keep in touch. They had Fam concerns humans would never understand.

Old dog knew most about the plans for building the City, and drew them a simple map with a claw, showing where they should continue to meet once they were down on Celta and outside the Ship.

Then the intercom blared: "Landing Sequence Imminent, please go to your secure seats."

To show his courage, Peaches waited for all the other Fams to run out of the park and to their landing nets before walking, tail up and waving, from the room. He curled the tops of his ears against the shrieking and pulsing warning, continued to saunter down Ship's corridors. People moved fast, running, panting.

Though his heart beat quick and hard, he ignored that to show *everyone,* human and Fam, his bravery.

Peaches, where ARE you! screamed his FamMan in demand.

On my way, he replied.

Translocating you...

NO! I'm coming! He hated moving through dimensional space. Scary on the ship, easier, maybe, on a planet. Maybe.

He'd only thought about the planet thing much and *OUTSIDE* except when he had to. So often, lately, he tried to hide the very scary thoughts.

So he loped the last meters to a new place Ship and Captain had opened up. They entered a round chamber, the Main Bridge. In the big chair in the middle Pilot sat.

FamMan Randolph led Grandma Chloe to her seat, a plush seat as befitted her status as one of the colonists who had paid for this trip, and as the Executive Officer of the Ship. He held her hands as she sat, then kissed both her cheeks.

"*Believe,*" he said aloud and let the word sing in their minds, backed the word with the complete faith *he* had. That the very smart Pilot and Ship would land them in a good place to live. That they *could* live on the new world. He, more than anyone on the Ship, knew about the planet.

"The Captain made me believe we could discover a wonderful new world and we did. Now believe me that we will live well on that world." Another squeeze of fingers with fingers. Peaches leapt up onto her lap and leaned against her and sent his purr into her bones.

We will need You, Grandma Chloe, he sent to her mind,

and she relaxed even more when she heard that, felt his sincerity.

"Yes, Grandmother, you are the head of our family. You know how to live on a planet. We need you, Peaches and me." One last kiss on her cheek, and Randolph began to pull the safety webbing over her. Peaches jumped down, stood on FamMan's feet to link better with him as they used their Flair magic to coat more safe spells on Chloe.

"I love you, Randolph, and Peaches," Chloe said in a firm voice.

I love you, too! Peaches replied, along with Randolph.

All around them people took their seats and strapped in and told each other of their love. The big feeling moving through this chamber, and like a huge wave through the Ship, inundated Peaches.

He still breathed fast.

When he reached FamMan's seat and his sling next to it, Peaches stopped.

Then, he just stood on shaking legs, shivering with fear. All his guts seemed to have knotted. He didn't want to live anywhere but here, where he ruled all the Fams, where he was comfortable, where he knew everything about everyone and everything.

For the first time, *ever*, he sent to his FamMan, *I am afraid.*

"Oh." FamMan scooped him up, held him close, cradled him and rocked him. Radiated love and comfort with the very warmth of his thoughts and body. Randolph had become stronger, emotionally, than Peaches had noticed. He didn't know when that had happened, but gratitude at Randolph's actions filled Peaches.

Randolph could be strong when Peaches felt weak.

Peaches didn't need to be strong all the time for Randolph or Grandma Chloe.

"It will be fine," Randolph crooned whispered.

Peaches knew what he meant. If Ship got in trouble and couldn't land, Pilot would blow them up and they wouldn't feel a thing, it would be so big and fast.

It will be fine, Peaches agreed.

After one last long and loving stroke, FamMan Randolph gently placed Peaches in his safety hammock, actually leaned down and kissed him on the nose. Peaches pretended to like that, though, and radiated love back to Randolph.

Randolph carefully placed Peaches in the sling. "I love you, Peaches."

I love you, FamMan Randolph.

After a last stroke from nose to tail, Randolph shut the sling and said Flair spell words. Then he took his seat just below and beyond Peaches' tail. Peaches' nose pointed toward the front of the bridge where the Pilot and Captain and Captain Lady sat.

He hung wrapped in a net hammock, kept reassuring himself he could tear it to bits and get out, if necessary.

"Here we go," Pilot said with great cheer.

The Ship *tipped*. Angled. Down. And his heart seemed to move around in his body and pumped fast, fast, fast.

And he had to admit to himself that deep in himself he'd lied all the time. To everyone, including himself. He couldn't imagine life on a planet. Didn't want to land. Didn't want to live anywhere but on Ship. Stupid to lie to self. Now he had to battle with his fear during the most dire circumstances of his life.

He had to believe. So he did. In his FamMan, who he

loved. In the love he felt for Chloe and FamMan, the love that helped him believe.

"Now leaving orbit," Pilot said.

"Affirmative," said the Ship. "We are in good position to land on the peninsula we chose."

Going down, down, down was nasty! Horrible fall, with air scrunching Peaches as if all his beautiful fat and muscles and bones should be together. Terrible. He opened his mouth a little and it got stuck that way!

FamMan and others gasped. Grandmother Chloe grimaced and slowly spit out words, "Gravity pressing against us as we enter. Three gravs, three times the amount of regular Earth gravities."

Peaches didn't like it, decided not to have any more truck with gravity.

Big fire streams of flowed across the portholes of the ship, like they were encased in fire. Someone screamed and more people did more and more and outside the command room.

Fams wailed in his mind.

Peaches breathed so quick darkness edged his vision. Blessed darkness.

He wrenched his head to look at Pilot.

She looked the same. Professional.

Did her fingers hover over the explode button?

Maybe.

Air squeezed around him so he couldn't breathe.

Blackness swallowed him.

⸙

SLOWLY PEACHES SURFACED to thinking instead of feeling.

Better to think, 'cause his whole body felt stomped on and wrung out.

And he felt *heavier.*

Helpless in the net! Gotta get out. Gotta get out!

Before he flailed and ripped the hammock, he remembered tug-open and closed his teeth around the string and yanked.

He fell from the sling and barely managed to twist and land on his feet. Hopping onto FamMan's lap, he stared at Randolph's slack face. His body felt limp, but Peaches could hear steady heartbeats, and FamMan breathed well. Peaches hesitated to wake him up.

Glancing over to Grandma Chloe, Peaches noted she looked shrunk. Little and whiter than usual with little brown spots on her face. He stared. Her hair seemed kinkier than usual, too. Odd.

A stifled moan echoed more in his head than in his ears, which still seemed to ring with swirling air pressures or winds inside the Ship or human mutterings or puppy howls above human hearing but too sharp in Peaches' ears.

He turned and saw Captain sitting before an also limp Captain Lady.

Oh, no! He rushed over, hopped onto Captain and licked the wet tracks on his face. Salty. *FamMan not awake yet, either. You did good, Captain. Captain Lady did good. Pilot did good. Not as good as Cats would have, but good.*

Most people stirred and stood, shaking their limbs. The puppy, thankfully, stopped yowling.

"The planet outside...Celta...is fully acceptable for Earth-human life." Ship announced. "Atmospheric pressure has been equalized. Opening all Landing Bays doors."

"Wait!" Captain ordered.

But Peaches heard all the doors of the Ship to *outside* open. Felt the air change again.

FamMan Randolph coughed and Peaches rushed back to him. Yes, his steps took more effort. Peaches licked and licked FamMan's face. *Just tired. You just a little tired, but time to wake up now.*

Blinking, then rubbing sticky sticky stuff from his eyes, FamMan opened his lashes and smiled at Peaches. "We're down." He looked toward the screens edging the bridge walls, then coughed. "Looks good. Ah, verdant."

Ship says We can live fine on planet! Just like You thought! Just like YOU said.

Randolph petted him. "Good, that's good." He moved his shoulders against the safety webbing. "A huge relief."

"Yessss," Peaches vocalized.

Grandma Chloe whimpered and Peaches jumped down from Randolph's lap and hurried over to her. FamMan moved a little slower, too, and Peaches reached her first.

Cocking his head, he opened his mouth for smell-taste and sensed her more with his Flair. *Help her, FamMan!* Peaches demanded.

After a moment's hesitation, Randolph unlocked Chloe's safety nets, lifted her small body into his arms and sat down again. Chloe stopped crying, leaned against her grandson and hugged him. "I've been so afraid. I didn't think I would actually make landfall. I thought I would die before we landed and never walk on solid ground again."

Ship had always felt plenty solid to Peaches.

A fascinating scent came to his nostrils, one that tempted. One from *outside.* He jerked as he realized that if he wanted to be First Paw Or Foot On Celta, he needed to move fast!

He shot toward the shut door of the Main Bridge leading to the corridor. *Come ON! I want out!* he insisted.

Randolph, hand-in-hand with Chloe, came up to stand near Peaches and said, "The Captain and his lady must go first."

Peaches huffed, prepared himself to lunge through the door as soon as it opened. But FamMan picked him up and he had to wait and watch as Captain and Captain Lady moved to in front of them. Both Chloe and Randolph bowed to the couple.

LET'S GO! Peaches yelled mentally.

The bridge doors opened and people stood in the hall, looking scared, holding belongings in sacks or boxes.

Peaches wiggled from Randolph's grasp and hopped down.

As Captain and Captain Lady proceeded down the hallway, following illuminated floor panels that Ship lit, the humans bowed to them.

And to him, Peaches, maybe. He trod close at their heels. And just behind him, the female puppy, still thinking she might be Fam to Captain Lady.

Soon they stood at the last door and looked at white sunshine angling into the huge bay.

They walked down the ramp to a wide space green with grasslike stuff, and stopped.

Peaches zoomed after them, the first Fam to put paw on the ground of the new planet! FamMan Randolph and Chloe joined him.

ZINGING SHOCK! Peaches hunkered down, ears flattened.

Flair magic surged from the dirt through his pads all the way to the tips of ears and tail.

Slowly he rose, and a breath that had seemed caught

inside him, all the way inside, coating the marrows of his very bones, rattled out of him on a cough. He smelled it—ship air in his lungs—that seemed to hang before him, then dissipated. When he drew in a breath, it brought a dizzying amount of new scents. Green and growing things headier than that of the Great Greensward itself.

He staggered, his paws crossing...his *eyes* crossing. Had to stand still to get his balance. Sliding his gaze around, he saw he was the only Fam standing.

Good. Little steps, kitten tip-toe pad steps.

The humans seemed to have it easier...and those recently been Awakened walked smoothly.

Grandma Chloe beamed a smile bigger than Peaches had ever seen on her face. Almost scary. She walked with a *bounce* in her step.

No, not truly scary. *Nothing, no thing,* scared him. All the fright he'd held inside for a long, long time had come out with that last breath containing Ship's air.

From the time Randolph had joined the conspiracy to take over the Ship and got them all in danger, to the terror of falling through space to land on this place that might kill them with that first breath.

To have such fear gone made him feel as exuberant as a kitten!

More peoples came and cried and laughed, then cheers filled the air.

He looked around, opened his mouth to curl his tongue in smell-taste sense. Chortled in glee.

Wonderful place! Tilting his head he stared at the sky not like the GreatGreensward sky and the trees and the bushes *more* and *wilder* around him than in the Ship's park. *Better.*

Flexing his claws, he dug them into the earth below,

smelled the new and fabulous smell of the planet, their home.

He opened his throat and yowled approval, shouting with his mind. *We have arrived on Celta!*

I HAVE ARRIVED!

= The End =

_____oo_____

NOTE: You can see more of Peaches in the story, Heart And Sword, in the collection titled Hearts and Swords. Please note, these stories, as well as the rest of the Celta books that feature Familiar Animal companions, are fantasy romances and not appropriate for children.

ZANTH GETS HIS BOY

This story was the result of requests by my readers and was previously published in my newsletter ONLY. Zanth essentially saved young Rand Ash's life as a child, and helped him mature to adulthood (backstory referenced in the first book of my fantasy romance series, HeartMate). By the way, for mature readers who want to follow up (or follow) Zanth, he appears on page 3 of the paperback, HeartMate. Complaining about the chef.

DRUIDA CITY, **Celta, 369 Years After Colonization, Spring**

Zanth, Fiercest Cat of Celta, Terror of Sewer Rats, *deserved* a rich life. Now that he knew what *rich* was.

In the market on the edge of Downwind, he'd smelled-tasted a plush flavor that whiffed through his nose and sank into his tongue. Unusual. So he followed the pant-legs of the man to find more of this goodness. Away from his Downwind alley and out, out, out! Past crowded city buildings, even.

To clean smelling places. Big houses with lots of land. No alleys.

The man went through a gate that smelled of bitter dog, and Zanth abandoned him to explore a wider area.

He looked into sheds and found one with a broken window that welcomed him. Warm and out of the late spring cold snap. Plump fuzzy cloth-covered things to sleep on. With tassels to play with, though they didn't taste too good.

Yes. *He deserved rich.*

Over the next couple of days, the sparse game around the shed concerned him, and, sniffing, he figured other Cats —though not smart like he—and raccoons and foxes also hunted in his new space. He ate adequately but not as good as he'd hoped. Muttered grumbly thoughts and cat hisses to himself.

Days got warmer, almost too warm in the shed, but nights continued cold enough to frost even his tough paw pads.

Wanting his favorite meal of sewer rat, he did one last sharpening of his claws on the wide door jamb leaving nice wide new wood instead of old boring stain. Yanked off and demolished the last tassel, and marked the whole inside as his. He'd come back later. Because he *deserved* rich.

He left the place that night to trot to the busier part of the city, then to Downwind where sewer rats ran free and abundant.

Soon enough he slunk along the narrow sort-of streets, noted the new odors at the nearest intersection a half block from his alley, then sauntered up to one of the few trash-throw-away pillar containers outside his home. It loomed tall above him, and no food spilled out. *Something* in there smelled really, really toothsome.

Sauntering in, he heard a hiss. Whirling, he confronted a rat!

While Zanth lounged in his shed place, a giant rat had moved into *Zanth's* alley!

Huge insult!

Nobody, no *rat* should be so unafraid of Zanth as to move into *his* space that he'd kept free from vermin and every-fliggering-one-else for *years*! How could this happen? Surely his reputation as the fiercest fighting Cat in Druida City should scare others away from his home for more than a few days!

Rat had the gall to raise his muzzle gums and show his big teeth at Zanth.

Last thing he'd do!

A quick fight later, with only a couple of nips and scratches, Zanth feasted on the dead rat. Regular alley rat and not sewer rat, and big, but not as savory as he wanted. Especially since good food odor wafted to him from the tall trash thing.

Slurp, slurp, slurp.

Belch.

Sigh and a little time to groom blood off whiskers before more munching.

A series of whimpers came from the deep, dark shadows at the end of the alley.

Zanth froze, fur bristling, head cocked so his best ear could hear. More, *sensed* the Other. Human and young. Zanth hurrumphed, stalked over to find a crying boy huddled in a corner. Should have noticed him before. He growled in his throat.

The boy flinched, shrank back when Zanth came close to study him, whiskers quivering. Though young, the boy looked large. Would grow to big man. As big to men as Zanth was to Cats. Zanth approved.

Dark hair, swarthy skin, light eyes.

Though the boy and his clothes and the big book he held smell-tasted scorched fire bad, and sewer ripe streaks, and a hint of pee, underlying all that lay the sweetness of *rich.* And when Zanth's whiskers touched the kit's skin, all Zanth's hair rose in tingling delight.

He smiled. The boy cringed. Smelled of big Flair-Magic. More Flair magic than Zanth had ever sensed from humans here Downwind. His nose twitched in remembrance of market days in nice part of city. Rich people *had* big Flair magic and could do big stuff.

Or big Flair magic people had rich.

So he sat and stared at the boy and revved his purr. The kit straightened, scrunched to the back alley wall through an unfortunate pool of rat piss. Then, tentatively, the boy reached out and stroked Zanth's head, all around it, under his ears, and he purred and purred and made it loud.

Then he heard words in his mind!

Greetyou, FamCat.

Zanth pondered the words, rubbing against one of the last rich-smelling portions of the boy's trous. The words in his head didn't sound much like those Zanth heard people say out loud in Downwind. And no one never said nothing to him in his head before. The boy's brain sparked with smart, like Zanth's. Smart magic Flair.

Greet, he said back to the boy.

I am Rand Ash, the boy said, then he panted wrenching wet breaths. His body shuddered. He made more of those little whimpering sounds like tiny kits did. Zanth hopped on him and licked his face, *nasty* slime, *great* boy.

Wetness came from the boy's eyes and nose and dribbled on Zanth. He cuddled closer so the stuff would fall on the boy's trous instead.

"Thank you," the boy, Rand Ash, said brokenly.

They sat for a while in silence, though drunk people walked across their alley entry. One man puked and others laughed.

Another cat stuck his head in, saw Zanth, jerked back. Looked again. Then, step by step, he snuck to the rat, set teeth into it, and hauled the carcass away.

Zanth didn't care. He sat on Flair rich boy. Besides, he'd eaten the best innards.

You hear my telepathic thoughts? said the boy mentally.

Yes.

Then you are a FamCat! An intelligent animal able to bond with people! Rand's thought zinged happy. Good. Always better than sad. *You are a Familiar Animal Companion! Maybe MY FamCat?*

That echoed sadness.

Boy might be in Downwind now, but came from rich, had big Flair, *would* be rich.

Yes, Zanth replied.

A choked shout of joy from the kit. He rose, and Zanth stood, reaching just below his knee.

The boy grabbed him under his front paws and hauled him up. Zanth dangled awkwardly. He didn't like it and grunted. "You are my FamCat!" Rand said. "My kitten."

Not kitten. Have big balls that work. YOU are MY FamBOY. MY KIT!

Yes, your FamBoy! Rand *shouted* mentally, making Zanth's brain ring. *We will be friends forever!*

All the boy's words reverberated through every nerve. Made Zanth feel good.

"And I will name you after..." Rand's voice cracked and shot out pain. A sniffling pause before he continued, *And I will give you an Ash Family name!* His mental tone squeaked high as a very young human kit's.

"Zanthoxyl," Rand said aloud. "Zanth!"

Huge sun-bright feeling burst inside Zanth, like he'd swallowed a lightspell! *Zanthoxyl, Zanth, Zanth, Zanth, Zanth, Zanth.* Six times he felt his name reverberate through him, finally said out loud by someone. From bones out, he'd always known his true name. And his boy did, too! Wondrous.

Flair magic working on them both.

Best We sleep here, Zanth said.

"Okay," Rand mumbled. Carefully, he used a cloth to clean a spot and placed the book there, then lay on his back, his arm around the book. In the next breath he dropped into sleep.

Stretched long, Zanth nearly matched his boy, *Rand,* in length. But Zanth didn't sleep that way. Instead he curled over chest and belly and cock, keeping Rand's vulnerable spots covered and warmed and protected.

Zanth snoozed.

Terror and horror stalked Rand's dreams, bled over into Zanth's joy of hunting sewer rats and crushed it. Nearly crushed *him,* his mind. He didn't let it, of course, but he whimpered with his boy's moans, saw the evil men burn down Rand's house and his family inside. Bad fire that once started would burn a body clear through, couldn't be stopped.

Saw the boy's mother turn from Rand, who'd been out of his bed and hidden, to try and save her husband and other children.

Zanth hissed. *His* boy, now. *His. He* would not abandon.

"Huh?" Rand sputtered, then coughed, turned on his side, opened wide eyes. "Bad dream, Zanth. Bad memories." He gave a sob. "Happened just tonight."

Really bad, Zanth agreed, licked his boy's face. *But you are not alone. I am with you.*

Thank you, Zanth FamCat, came the fading thought and the kit fell asleep again.

=^..^=

When the sun speared watery fingers into the alley the next morning, Zanth showed Rand the corner to piss in, and the drip from the water spout to drink from. Rand put his hands under the drip and said Words that buzzed along Zanth's fur. His skin looked cleaner.

Then he sat, hunched forlornly and stared at Zanth. Mouth trembling, he told Zanth, "Enemies firebombed my home and burned it, and my Family." His breath caught. "That really happened." Now his whole face scrunched and his voice hitched with tears "All...all...my Family is gone. M... my fa-father, m...my bro-thers, N...Nuin...Gwy...Gwydion. M.... Ma...Mama!" His voice wailed, then he put a fist over his mouth as he looked around the alley, out at the street.

Zanth rotated his ears, strained his hearing, said, *No one here.*

The boy crumbled to the ground and cried a long, long, time. Minutes, even.

Zanth brushed against him again and again, until the quiet, wet sounds stopped. *I am here, with you.*

Yes, thank you, Zanth, Rand returned telepathically.

I will stay with you.

Good. The boy fisted his red-rimmed eyes. "You killed the awful rat."

"Yessss," Zanth said aloud. Only a few smart Cats like him could do that. He stretched, feeling the bites and scratches. All healing.

His voice yet small, Rand said, "And you kept me warm last night."

"Yessss." Zanth licked a paw and groomed his ears, the one with the scars and the other ragged one.

Rand's words and feelings came in Zanth's head. *And you saved me from my horrible memories and dreams.*

"Yesss," aloud, then, *Me hero.* He leaned over and swiped a tongue on his boy's hand.

A couple of more snuffles that turned to sniffs. "I'm hungry, what's that smell?"

New food in trash thing.

"Oh. Is is good to eat?"

Mostly tastes good.

"Uh, sanitary?"

Not know that word.

"I s'pose it doesn't matter," Rand muttered. "Mama..." His lips trembled. He stood and sucked in a breath, made a fake smile at Zanth. "Let's go."

Zanth stood and flicked his tail. *Follow Me, kit.*

He took the boy to the nearby trash compost pillar, tall as two Rands and fatter than the boy with roundness. Rand murmured spells to open it and get better food. Boy was good for something.

A few minutes later, Rand gave Zanth a shy smile, and they shared the not-too-old furrabeast steak leftovers, some clucker bites.

"We're lookin' for a boy," a man's voice boomed down the cross-street. "Lost FirstFamily boy. Big for six years of age." Pause. "Mebbe gotta book. One'a them fancy old-time books."

"Reward?" snapped old woman Zanth had heard called Brevipes.

A clearing of a throat. "A'course."

Zanth opened his mouth and curled his tongue, drew in a big breath. *Bad man. Bad! Run!*

He loped away.

Rand stood still, hiding behind the tall trash thing. *No,* he said. *Do not run. I must pretend to be part of here. Downwinder.*

Yes! Zanth paused. He had not shown well. He angled his head and eyes to look at the boy, small enough to stand stiff behind the trash composter and not be seen. Eyes wide, face a mask of fear.

He *looked* rich. And now Zanth worried. The puny amount of black fur on Rand's head didn't look like other Downwind boys. His nose looked straight, but Zanth figured boy-fights would fix that.

You stay here, I will go and see this BAD man.

No! Rand yelled in his mind.

Zanth ignored him, swaggered up to the man. Who smelled sort of rich and all mean.

The old woman looked down at him, cackled. "Hello, tomcat, you fliggerin' nuisance."

He ignored her and her stupid words. Stared up at the man.

"Huh," Brevipes said. Narrowing her eyes, she went on. "Some ructions and crying going on last night in your alley, tomcat. Mebbe—"

"Crying?" snapped the man. "Where's the cat's alley?"

Lifting a crooked hand, she pointed a gnarled finger. "Right there. An' ain't there someone behind that composter?"

The man shot forward. Zanth tried to tangle his legs, got kicked.

Flinging his arms upward in spell-wave, the mean man yelled, "Find, translocate boy spell!" Invisible scary Flair rippled through the air, Zanth saw his boy tumble, yanked from behind the trash pillar and into the open, arms and legs thrashing. He screamed as he was drawn to the laughing man. A guy who sweated fighting-killing-anticipation.

Zanth's *boy kit!*

He jumped to Rand's back as the boy zoomed by, then used Rand's Flair and the evil's Flair and his *own* Flair to hop up on the man's shoulder.

"Gotcha!" The man grabbed Rand.

GOTCHA! Zanth screamed in fury, biting and tearing the guy's ear. *His* turn to shriek.

Zanth loosed his bladder. The guy swore, fell.

"Free!" Rand yelled. He stumbled away. Zanth found himself zipped through the air and into Rand's clasp. The boy began to run.

"Kill him!" the man yelled, pulling a blazer.

Rand ran, leapt to one side. The blazer hit the composter and trash went everywhere, rolling crap along the street behind them and other men showed up and jumped around, also shooting.

The boy dodged, sped even faster.

"Wait, you owe me a reward!" Brevipes shrieked.

"Fliggering flitch. Not unless we catch him, we don't."

Another blazer stream missed, but a spell came in its wake that made Zanth's paws tingle.

Using huge effort, Zanth teleported them a couple of blocks. Out of the commotion. They lost the evil men hunting them.

=^..^=

They spent the rest of the day hiding, this time on the nicer edge of Downwind where it met the rest of the city. Places where humans ate, with good, full trash compost receptacles. Zanth and Rand gorged. Rand did *cleansing spells* on his clothes while Zanth watched. Then the boy left the rich clothes in place of other, bigger boy clothes that looked like garments Zanth often saw. He gave a last sniff of the richness and only looked back once when they walked away, his paws tingling off and on.

As the sun set behind the low roofs of Downwind, Zanth said, *Me know better place. You help Me find more food when We get to shed.*

"Huh," Rand said, then pulled pieces of meat off the slightly burnt clucker and tossed them to Zanth. He'd gotten more meat off the bird than Zanth had managed. Fingers could be helpful, Zanth saw.

When they'd eaten their fill that evening, they wound their way north, out of the worst of Downwind. Zanth led the boy toward the big houses and land and Zanth's shed. After a while, Rand seemed to know the way. When Zanth's paws got cold, Rand stooped and picked him up.

Zanth directed the boy to Zanth's shed. Rand stopped several paces away, coughed. "What is that awful smell?"

Zanth snarled, *Boy knows nothing. Has bad taste,* smacked Rand with a sheathed-claw paw.

Rand dropped him.

Trotting up to the little building. Zanth sniffed in his own scent, and other nasty-cleanser stuff.

Growling, he circled the shed. No opening showed where he could get in. No broken window, no cracked threshold or board, no crumbling hole in the permacrete. And Zanth's boy shivered with cold.

Zanth might lose him before they became rich.

Terrible thought!

Rand looked around. "I don't recognize this estate. Minor noble?"

"The tracking spell on the cat worked. There's the Ash kid! Back in Noble Country, like you said!" yelled a man, jumping from a bush. Blazer rays only missed Zanth because Rand 'ported him into his arms.

Boy panted with low shaky moans. Chest rising, falling fast. *'Porting!* his mind screamed at Zanth.

Noooo! Zanth cried. Too late. Mind flashed question where they'd end up, Rand's burnt out house?

They landed in the alley.

More shouts!

"Team one, they're back!" The shout sounded in Zanth's mind along with his ears. Fear shot through him. "Rue was right, follow that cat!"

'Port over the back wall. Looks like this! Zanth pushed a strong image into boy's mind.

He squeaked. They vanished. Landed hard in smelly puddle in other alley.

RUN! Zanth yelled. *Run south to deep slums. We will lose them. They follow, they get beat up!*

Rand ran. Zanth ignored the boy's wet eyes and drippy nose, more sob breathing. They ran until the wild fear left and exhaustion came. To the warrens, mostly narrow alleys here. Many living in lean-tos, crates.

Shuffling now, Rand drooped. Zanth hopped from his loose grip and walked in front of the boy, tail waving. He knew this area.

Rand glanced at the alley they passed. Slowed. "There's a nice big crate there. And light. A water spout, too. No cracked pavement. Sorta clean. Better than many I've seen. No rats?"

The alley is too big. Zanth informed him. *I cannot defend it. Good barrow-tunnel not too far away.* He paced on a few body lengths before noticing Rand had stopped.

I like this, Rand's words came to Zanth's mind along with

a rush of stubborn determination. Rand wiped his nose on his sleeve.

With a gusty breath, Zanth turned. Sauntered back and scrutinized the alley. He'd prefer a burrow. *Too big, CAN'T defend!*

YOU can't defend it. I can. WE can.

Sitting and blinking, Zanth stared up at him. *You are right, boy.*

Rand, your FamBoy, he corrected.

"Yesss," Zanth agreed, stalked into the alley he and his boy owned now. *Crate is good. You fix to keep out cold and hot and rats. We will live fine.* When Rand caught up with him, he jumped into Rand's arms.

"We will live good enough," said Rand. "Someday we will find or build a good shed."

Someday We will be rich.

Though the boy still held him with gentle arms, Zanth *felt* rage flash through him, through them. Saw bad seeing of bad fire and heard echoes of harsh words. "Yes, Zanth. We will get my fortune and title back and rebuild my Residence. We will be rich." Oddness covered Rand and moved over Zanth, too, like a spell. Spellwords. Vow.

Zanth began to slip from his boy's arms and Rand hitched him up, looked into his eyes. As Zanth watched, wetness vanished from Rand's eyes and his mouth went from straight to curved.

"Love ya, Zanth. We do this together."

Love you, FamBoy. We will be rich together. Life is good.

=The End =

PINKY BECOMES A FAM

*Another story requested by readers. Pinky (of a beige/cream color like Peaches), changed from a regular cat to a Familiar Companion during the story **Heart Choice.** I didn't describe that since it didn't affect the main romance between Straif T'Blackthorn and Mitchella Clover. But it was a question of "how" that teased at readers (and me), so here it is.*

Druida City, Celta, 404 Years After Colonization, Spring

Pinky sunk his claws into the examination table in the little white room. He raised his fur. He'd act tough and others wouldn't see how scared he was.

He'd told his Boy that he wanted to become a Familiar Companion.

Dimly he understood a Familiar Companion was more. More thinking-being, but more closeness and love, too. He wanted that. He and his Boy deserved that. But it would be hurt and hard.

The beautiful and wise human female who could make him Fam looked down at him now as her hand traveled over his back, rounded along his tail. He flicked it and she smiled and he liked looking at her better.

"Now, Pinky, tell me why you want to become a FamCat?"

He heard a word he knew…"FamCat." He sat and stared at her. Her face fell into disappointment. He looked at his Boy who stood in a corner of this small and scary room. His Boy shifted from foot to foot and opened his eyes wide. Then the puny bits of fur over his Boy's eyes dipped.

Oh! Pinky knew that expression. He remembered another word, one the female had just spoken. "Why."

Like, *Why WOULD you eat that bug? Why DO you run from the waterfall shower?* He saw those scenes in his head with his Boy's face the same. Question. Yes, the voice went up, *question.*

He sat tilted his head so his gaze met the good woman's. "Mew."

Her eyefur went down, too, she put one hand—not as big as many hands—on his head, wrapped the other around his upper torso.

And he…he *felt* her. In his head! Yes, in his head. Warm and good and soft and loving! Oooooh! And she smelled so good, with a hint of catnip. He purred hard.

Why do you want to become a FamCat? Mostly words pinged in his mind, but he got images in his head. Zanth, the big, FamCat, who thought he was the best, swaggering, sneering. *Zanth talking in his head with his FamMan who gave him PRETTIES.* Yes, Pinky could hear at the bottom of his ears when Fams talked with their peoples.

Zanth lived in this place. Pinky growled.

The next cat who showed up in his mind was that Drina. The little cat as big as Pinky. Who lived in the same house as he did and talked to her man. She also thought she was the best. She hid behind doorways and swatted Pinky in the butt when he walked by. Every. Day. To show him *she* was better. She wasn't! He hissed.

Then he saw in his head a long-haired sweet female gray tabby cat. That cat lived here in this house, too. But she was not Fam. She did not talk to this female who stroked Pinky now, who was her woman. She thought of nothing but pretties and eating and sleeping in the sun and love. Pinky huffed a breath. He was *not* like her.

He stared deep, deep into the woman's eyes so she would *know* he was *more than* cat.

The woman nodded at Pinky, her face serious.

More words and less visions from the woman, he thought he felt her stir up stuff in his mind, the back, or maybe the bottom. It felt funny, tickled *inside* his head. Made his blood fizzy, and his eyes weird and his ears hum. He felt a big pulse of his magic surge through him. He coughed, then purred in pleasure.

"Why do you want to be a FamCat, Pinky?" Her mouth said the words out loud where his ears angled to hear.

He showed her scenes. Of meowing to his Boy and his Boy not understanding, then a new-future-event where he lay around his Boy's neck and his fur touched skin and they shared interest in bugs, and birds, and skirls and they didn't have to use stupid sounds to talk. And Pinky knew right away what *FamCat* and *Why* meant. Most of all he thought of his love for his Boy, projected that. Got love *back* from his Boy in the corner and they shared it all.

The female picked him up in her soft hands and looked him in the eyes. "I *believe* you can achieve your quest, Pinky. That you can become a FamCat You have Flair, psi power, in you. It just needs to be...drawn from the pool inside you to stream and be used."

He heard "FamCat," but he felt everything else.

"You are smart," she said, and he learned from her touch what *smart* meant. He *was* a smart Cat. Smart as humans. As smart as that snotty cat who bullied him, that Drina.

Yesss. Smart enough and with enough dammed magic inside him that he could be Fam. Remove the shadows obscuring his thoughts. Open a passage to his Flair-magic flow. Then he would reach his greatness. No more swats from Drina and much love from all peoples who liked Fams.

"You are a strong cat. You can pass any challenge. You can become a Fam. You can do it," she said in a happy voice.

Yes. He could do it.

=^..^=

The challenges began.

Zanth hulked on heavy paws toward Pinky, upper muzzle lifted to show a fang. Pinky hunkered down, not understanding why he'd been put here in this small and empty round room with a wooden floor—obviously *Zanth's* territory. Was this how he became a Fam? By fighting cats three times his size?

"Grrrr." He rose slightly, balanced on his paws, ready to spring. Ready to fight Zanth. *Ready* to be Fam.

Then the big mean Zanth, who acted like he owned the world, jumped faster and longer than Pinky thought possible and hit him and sent him rolling.

He rose with a hiss, hurting at the left shoulder, saw Zanth parading around the room, tail in the air, nose lifted, looking at a window where peoples watched them.

Pinky's Boy did not stand with them and Pinky's heart hurt. The wonderful woman's eyes looked sad, her mouth turned down.

Then he *heard*—did he?—heard... The whish of air and scent of cat warned him and he hopped to the side just in time for Zanth to miss him by a whisker. *Move right, avoid left forepaw strike!* He jumped, swiped out himself. But a couple of those claws pierced him and he knew red blood spotted his beige fur. Boy's older female-Dam-person liked the color of Pinky's fur. El-e-gant, she said.

His ribs pained him now, too.

Wait! He was *thinking, instincts being SLOWED.* Wait. Think while Zanth struts some more. Ha! Zanth's ear showed bloody. Don't preen. Think. Pinky scrubbed a paw across muzzle and right eye. Zanth should have slashed with right paw, but had done left. Pinky had known Zanth would use left *before* he'd hit. Thoughts, images, rattled in Pinky's head and he shook it and the pictures tilted and looked less flat and got substance...and though Zanth didn't face Pinky, he saw the black tip of that cat's tail twitch and went on alert.

Zanth *teleported.* And whirled. And, all claws flexed, fangs showing, *leapt* at Pinky.

He twisted away, zipped sideways, pivoted and hopped up high, high, high to light on Zanth's back, dug in with own claws. Zanth yowled! Pinky snarled in triumph.

Another image came to mind. How Zanth planned on ramming Pinky next...he missed his bite to Zanth's tail, rolled off and *when* that cat rushed straight at him, zoomed under his belly and out through the bigger cat's bowed back legs, wheezing a laugh. But he *knew* now. Knew why this mean alpha cat fought him.

Well, Zanth liked fighting. Who didn't?

But he also *projected* stuff, Zanth pictures, to Pinky. To *teach.* And make Pinky scared just because he could.

Pinky could see those pictures. So *he* shouted, from his

head to Zanth's, and shrieked out loud at the same time. *You STOP!*

An amazed expression crossed Zanth's face as his paws *did* stop and the rest of him slid across the floor. He had to scramble with scritching paws and claws to avoid the wall.

Pinky smirked. Sat and glanced aside and dampened his paw and groomed his whiskers.

From half-closed eyes, he observed the peoples standing in the window. Zanth's big FamMan, the Very Big Guy, stood with arms crossed, a curl at one end of his mouth. Wonderful lady grinned with pride at Pinky. Two other shadows just stood. He sniffed long and hard but did not smell those peoples.

Grrrrr.

Now Zanth stalked to Pinky on soft paw pads, a fake smile on his muzzle.

Pinky did the fake smile, too.

Zanth stopped, slowly arched his back, raising his fur—

And the lady appeared in the middle of the room. She clapped her hands. "This test and exploration of Flair and stimulating Pinky's Flair is over."

Pinky didn't know *exploration.* He understood his name, easy. He heard and comprehended *Flair*—mind magic to do stuff. Cocking his head he felt for the idea of *stimulating* from the lady and got it.

Yes, she tried to make his magic Flair more.

Good.

He tried a word that came to his mind and his tongue, but his mouth could not say aloud. A word that peoples said when someone came up to them. He sent it out from his mind. *Greetyou, lady.*

Zanth growled.

Then the lady held Pinky. Her Flair had 'ported him to

her. He turned his head to sneer at Zanth but she said in words that ruffled Pinky's fur with her breath and from her mind to his, *Greetyou, Pinky.*

He opened his mouth to pant pain away and she made a noise and stroked him and then his pain stopped. That's why all Fams loved her. She Healed them.

Ready for your next trial? she asked him with a thought-and-words.

"Yesssss," he said really out loud.

Zanth threw a hissy fit.

=^..^=

Another challenge, trial. More exploration and stimulation of his Flair. Pinky hoarded the new words, sounded them in his mind as his ears had heard them. Peoples words attached to pictures in his brain he recognized.

Another different room. This one had some furniture and thick rugs and the place smelled mostly of Zanth's human Family and some of Zanth and some of the other cat with no Flair.

"Princess is my cat," the lady said when she lowered Pinky to the floor. He stuck his paws out so he stood, though he trusted the lady enough that he could lie at her feet. "My name is Danith D'Ash."

Dan-ith Dash, he said with his mind, though this thinking out loud hurt some.

Rain spit against the long windows and the lady glanced there and sighed. "I had some outside tests planned. Get out in the fresh air."

He did not know the word, but Pinky thought the image at Danith—Flair-mind-magic blanket that kept peoples dry, Fams and humans.

"A weathershield spell," she informed him. "But that won't keep the landscape dry since we didn't erect one over the area." Then she got an image of her mate and said with her thoughts, *Rand can you...*

Pinky only heard and understood the first part, so he practiced the new words in his head. *Weath-er-shield spell.*

She put blocks of wood before him and some thick glass stuff, too. Pinky's eyes widened. He was not allowed near glass stuff.

"These are puzzles. The wood blocks make shapes. I will send you the shape I want and you will arrange the blocks." She squatted down, flicked her teeny finger claw against the class and it made a pretty noise that made his ears angle. "After the blocks, I will play a tune on these tumblers. You will repeat the tune for me. Then I will *think* of the sounds I want and you will play the tune for me."

Pinky heard and remembered the new words, associated them with ideas. He sat solidly on his rump. *Ready.*

So he rearranged blocks this way and that, slowly with his paws, as shapes formed in his head.

Then the lady—Danith—would mix them up fast with her hands. Humans had clever hands but bad claws. No peoples watched him from outside the windows in the rain, but he felt eyes on him. He thought the house must know the fall of his paws and the size of his body and that he visited. He hadn't made up his mind about FamHouses yet. He didn't think the one he lived in now should let Drina hit him in the butt.

"Pinky, pay attention! Let's do the music memory test."

So he played with pings on the glasses and it didn't matter that his claws scratched the glass. He felt like little explosions went off inside his mind, yes, painful but he sat up very straight when Danith laughed and petted his head *with two hands* and said she was proud of him.

After that he had lunch with Zanth FamCat—who made snide mind comments as he ate messily—and the regular cat who walked in dragging sparkley collars on the floor. *She* couldn't fight. But Pinky hid his own scorn of Prin-cess because Danith loved the cat and he liked Danith.

He sucked up a lot of water, too, the morning had been hard.

When lunch ended, Danith picked him up and held him and that soft and animal loving and wonderful aura enveloped him and he relaxed against her. She smelled *so* good, like catnip and food and sleeping on a thick rug in the spring sun.

They went through a door into a huge room. So high Pinky couldn't really see the ceiling. Or maybe the ceiling was tinted black. In front of him stood a narrow opening between walls. He gazed up. He *might* be able to jump as high as the walls...if he could use a little boost from his Flair-magic, but they seemed too narrow to sit on comfortably.

His breath caught and his throat tightened and he squeaked. *He was thinking of using his FLAIR!*

Then he let a pleased and surprised purr rumble out of him.

"Go on, Pinky," Danith said, "Go through the maze."

He stared up at her and she smiled her beautiful smile but didn't tell him anything more but he knew it would be all right. Ears angled, whiskers at alert he stepped into the corridor and walked along until he came to a branching path.

A sheer whistle attracted his attention and he glanced

up to see a green bird perched on one of the corners of the wall. *Go to the right,* came a whispery voice in his mind.

Right?

The bird clicked its beak in an annoyed way and lifted one wing and pointed.

Pinky sniffed and took that path.

Barely squeezed to one side fast enough to miss the stinky poop the bird let loose as it flew over him, cackling.

You should have thanked her, Danith scolded in his head.

THANK YOU! he yelled from his head.

Nobody said nothing.

He continued prowling forward, ears tilting as he listened hard, tail waving. At the next junction, he heard a couple of solid thumps, smelled Zanth to his *right,* but thought that cat lurked around the corner. A hoarse grumble hit his mind, *Come to Me, little kitty!*

Oh, no, he wouldn't. He looked the other way and saw a white and black chubby housefluff with those stupid long ears.

Come here, LEFT, the housefluff said. A housefluff knew *left* and could speak well, when Pinky couldn't! Not okay!

He kept a nice smile on his muzzle, though and when he reached the hopping creature he paused to lick its nose and projected gratitude, *Thank you.*

He told himself it didn't matter that the fluffy thing didn't answer him.

Every time he came to a turn he'd meet a different FamAnimal who would talk to him in his head...a fox, a dog with smelly breath, even a kitten. Go *left* or *right.* He always said *Thank you,* but none of them responded.

When he reached the end of the maze, Danith smiled at him and held out her arms.

Sure enough, he could use his Flair to jump into them.

"You did very, very well, with all the mind tests," she said. "You are becoming a Fam."

She nuzzled him but by the time she put him back on his paws, his relief made him dizzy.

"One last thing," she said.

He tensed.

A loud noise behind him made him jump and he whirled to see all the walls had vanished. Now he stood in the middle of a big round room with holes near the bottom of the walls, and platforms of all sorts up and down the walls, and some cubbyholes. He saw the bird on a perch, eating seeds and ignoring him. He saw the fox and the housefluff and the kitten in a pile of kittens and the drooling dog. He blinked and he knew this terrible place.

All of these peoples were Fams. And none of them had a Boy like Pinky did.

He was in the a-dopt-ion cen-ter. He was so lucky.

Danith gestured. "Just say hello."

So he set his paws, swept his gaze around without meeting eyes, and shouted, *GREETYOU, FAMS!*

They all yelled back, making the noise of their hellos, too. Barks, different from fox to wolf to dog, the horrible screeching of birds, all sorts of cat acknowledgments—mews and meows and purrs and...

And they all started bellowing in his head.

Pinky, pinky, pinky! the kittens squealed in a variety of shrill voices that hurt inside and out. They hopped up and down in their box on the floor, paining his eyes as he tried to keep track of them.

The dog began to howl. Badly.

He let his head drop, his tail droop. His paws sweated and sweated but dizziness didn't let him wash himself so he could cool down. He collapsed in the middle of the room with all those Fams eyes fixed on him. Yowls and meows, clamoring cries and yips assaulted his sensitive ears. Many, many voices high and squeaky to low and rumbly, battered the inside of his head until it throbbed.

All of him throbbed and throbbed and throbbed from eartip to claw...along with every beat of his heart.

The horrible babble reached a screeching pitch in his head where he couldn't think, but each word felt like a fiery thread. New words and ideas and notions and whole phrases and sentences tumbled like rocks in a landslide in his mind.

He couldn't take it. One more second would drive him crazy!

He got out of there and landed, panting, on the examination room table. He curled up tight and put his paws over his head.

The door opened a couple of minutes later and the smell of Danith rushed into the room.

"What a *fantastic* cat you are, Pinky. *What a FAM.* You *teleported.*"

He wished she'd whisper.

But then her soothing hands petted him, stroked and banished his weariness, and he heard the quiet in the room and nobody screamed in his head. He moved a paw away from one of his eyes. He caught her concerned expression before she met his gaze and flicked a smile on. "You've lost some weight."

Rolling over, he tried to sit up and she helped him. His fur felt a little too slick with...he didn't know what. Ick.

With a long sweep of her hand, she cleaned him up and banished his weariness. He sighed and leaned against her.

Thunk. The door swung open. Zanth strolled in. Pinky stiffened.

I did what you said, FamWoman, said Zanth, and gave Danith a fake-sweet smile. *I did the fight with the puny cat.* He sniffed. *I did the maze. I did everything you asked.* He sat straight and puffed out his fur, gaze fixed on Danith. *I deserve cocoa mousse.* The fake-sweet smile widened into a sickening-happy grin. *As big as my head!* Zanth ended.

Then Zanth's FamMan, the Very Big Guy, strode in. "Here you are." He kissed Danith. When he stepped back he frowned down at Pinky.

Who stared right back up at him. *Greetyou.*

Very Big Guy grunted.

"Rand T'Ash," Danith murmured.

So. T'Ash—and now Pinky got all sorts of memories from all sorts of peoples about that name—had grunted.

"People," Danith corrected. "It's not peoples, it's always 'people.'"

Zanth sat and licked a forepaw, groomed his ear. *Peoples is fine.*

A knock came at the door and Pinky's heart leapt. His Boy had arrived!

"Come in," Danith called.

"Greetyou, Danith. Greetyou, T'Ash. Greetyou, Zanth," Pinky's Boy said. "Thank you for sending your glider for me." But he didn't look at them, he looked at Pinky, who sat up even straighter than Zanth, full of pride.

His boy gasped and charged forward and Danith stepped aside.

"He *is* a *Fam* now. I can see it in his eyes! We will be able to talk to each other telepathically! *Greetyou, Pinky.*

Time to really use his new mind-voice Flair. *I...am...PINKY!* he announced.

Everyone smiled except Zanth, who snorted. But Pinky liked the sound of his mental voice, nice and deep.

His Boy scooped him off the the table and cuddled him. "I *heard* him. Did you hear him? I have a FamCat now. Can I take him to T'Blackthorn's?"

Another fact rose from deep in his brain to ping in his mind. *His Boy was called ANTENN.*

Pinky said, *I want to be with you now, Antenn.*

"Yes! Thank you, thank you, thank you, Danith!" Antenn said, nearly hopping.

"I'll go with you," Danith said decidedly. "No one will doubt me." She kissed her husband, put a hand on Antenn's shoulder, and opened the door.

"Until later, Pinky," T'Ash said.

Pinky remembered manners. *Merry meet.*

"And merry part," said T'Ash.

And merry meet again, Pinky said with his mind and Antenn said aloud.

Good-bye and go away now, said Zanth, then jumped on T'Ash's shoulder. *FamMan, time for mousse!* Zanth licked his chops.

=^..^=

Antenn talked and talked as they rode back to the smart House where they lived while Antenn's adopted Dam worked with pretty fabric and tinting and furniture there. The man who owned the House was having a large party and a ritual this evening—and Pinky understood all of those concepts.

"Yes, I know about the party and ritual," Danith said. "Rand and I will attend."

Pinky lay on Antenn's lap, purring. "Now you tell me all about the changing-into-a-Fam process."

With much stumbling and slow words, Pinky did, and

got a little shock when Antenn told him that what Pinky had thought had passed in one day, had really occurred over three. Pinky had no recollection of that, but when he probed his memory found dark spots like he'd just passed out from exhaustion.

Danith murmured, and stroked him now and then, too, and he decided he didn't mind those dark times left in his head.

The glider stopped and the door raised and Antenn hopped out and ran with Pinky toward the front doors. Pinky rather liked the jogging, *did* like the closeness with his FamBoy. "Residence," Antenn yelled at the house, and that word fit like a puzzle piece in Pinky's head. What the smart Houses were called, Residence.

"Yes, Antenn?" the House said, in real words, because it had magic, too. Pinky thought it could put words in his head, too.

That is correct. Welcome, FamCat.

"Pinky is a Fam!" Antenn said. Sometimes he was a little slow.

Congratulations, Pinky, the Residence said and it echoed and Pinky knew it talked to him, and Antenn and Danith and Antenn's Dam who walked toward them with grace nearly like a cat's, smiling. The adopted Dam's hair looked like fire and light caught it and Pinky admired it.

"Congratulations, Pinky!" caroled the Dam who didn't have much Flair. "I'm so glad he managed to become a Fam. Now we can all talk together."

"Thank you, Mitchella," said Antenn.

Thank you, Mitchella, repeated Pinky.

Antenn ran up to her and they hugged, Pinky between them. She was very soft. Pinky liked this hug the very best.

Then Man-of-Many-Place-Smells, who the House

owned, walked up to them and Mitchella stepped away. Pinky met the guy's steady gaze and he reached out and knuckle-scrubbed Pinky on the head. "Congratulations, Pinky."

Thank you, Pinky said. He did not know what other humans called this guy.

Man-of-Many-Place-Smells turned to Danith. "Do I owe—"

"Absolutely nothing. Helping Pinky was my pleasure."

"Right. I want to thank you, also, for you and T'Ash coming tonight."

"We wouldn't miss it."

"Later." And he teleported away so smoothly and easily that Pinky envied his big Flair.

Mew. The snotty Drina descended the staircase with much posing to show off how pretty she thought she was. *Oh,* she said. *It's Danith D'Ash, my very good friend.* The FamCat sauntered over to Danith and stropped her ankles. Pinky suppressed his hair that wanted to raise. Danith had helped him *more,* been with him more, been a better friend. He even refrained from sniffing, though he felt better when he saw Danith hide a smile as the petted the cat three times, then straightened.

"I need to return now and dress. We'll be back soon." She hugged Antenn's Dam who hugged her and held on a little bit. Those two acted like litter mates though no common blood ran through their veins. Danith left.

As soon as the door closed behind her, Drina presented Pinky with her butt and sashayed down the entry hall, tail moving a sinuous, disdainful way.

Pinky *teleported* to land right behind her, swiped at her and missed her butt but got a glancing blow on her tail.

She hop-turned, arched her back and hissed.

Pinky didn't back down. *I am Fam, too, snotty cat. I can use my Flair to move around, too!* He showed his fangs. *If you hit me in the rump again you WILL regret it.*

Common Cat! She spit at him but he sent it back to her face and she squealed and vanished.

He swaggered back to a bent over and laughing Antenn, and a tear-running laughing Mitchella. The House creaked like it laughed, too.

Mitchella swung him up and kissed him on the nose, stepped close to Antenn and they *both* held him. Pinky purred.

He had a FamBoy, Antenn, and a FamWoman, Mitchella. And they had him, Pinky the FamCat.

= The End =

ZANTH CLAIMS TREASURE

This is the oldest of my stories, and the shortest. You can find it in a couple of versions all over the internet, including my blog. I put it in my first newsletter. The story came to me while writing Heart Journey. I kept wondering how Del Elecampane, a map maker always on the road, managed to get T'Ash to sell her Landscape Globes in his jewelry store in Druida City. Answer: Fams were involved. Del's fox, and the FamCat Zanth, of course.

Celta, 407 Years After Colonization, Summer

Zanth's whiskers twitched. The smell was incredible. Incredible and wonderful and with the scent of great Flair magic.

He padded warily through the night and the bushes that rose high above his head. He'd never been out of the city of Druida before. Here on his FamMan's overgrown southern estate there were creatures that might try and make a mouthful of him. But he was a canny and clever cat, the preeminent cat of Druida, and therefore, of course, the whole world of Celta.

The bushes loomed and rustled with animals and

midnight noises. He placed each paw carefully, flexed his claws.

Treasure pulsed up ahead and he meant to have it.

Slithering under the rusted greeniron gate, he wallowed for a few instants in the dirt and dust, spreading his own scent. Notifying all in the area that the mighty Zanth was on the prowl, that this estate, once abandoned, belonged to *him*.

He sniffed luxuriously. No celtaroons. He'd cleaned out two nasty nests in the few days they'd been here. Wolf scent drifted from far away, but the pack consisted of low, unintelligent creatures and no match for Zanth.

He was a FamCat of the highest order, of the greatest nobility. Now he was pampered, and that was absolutely his due. He'd found the boy child, Rand T'Ash, in the slum of Downwind and cared for him, let Rand love him and be a Familiar companion.

Then they grew big enough to walk the Vengeance Stalk. They'd killed those men who'd murdered Rand's Family. Zanth had gotten his Residence and his room and his bed and his velvet pillow.

And his chef.

Rumor lied that Zanth was soft and fat. He could still take any feral tom in Druida City.

The tantalizing scent came from beyond the ragged gliderway...it came from the road. Not a big road, but one with lots of odors of stridebeasts, llamas, a horse or two. And predator and prey animals and carrion eaters.

The lake to the south ladened the air with rich smells of fish and small prey and his favorite, sewer rat.

But even wet rat didn't smell as good as this human-Flair-made-thing.

He sauntered out, nose lifted, reveling in all the excellent new smells, the slight breeze sliding against his fur, the beingness in a new place just waiting for him to put his paw prints all over it.

In a few bounds he found the sphere. Glass with interesting-unique-special stuff floating inside. It smelled of woman and strange places beyond any Zanth had experienced. He recognized a little tang of the Great Platte Ocean, and of Gael City where he'd been, and even an icy wind from the far north that caused him to shiver and his fur to rise. More recently was the gaminess of the Hard Rock Mountains.

The orb was slightly buried in dirt. He pawed it out, grinning as his claws dug deep in the rich earth of this new place that would know him.

He rolled the sphere a little way, watching something sparkle inside it. Tasting it, his tongue absorbed some of the Flair that created it and emanated from it and he purred. It made him feel better. A treasure indeed.

That is MINE. The snarling shout, mental and physical, stopped Zanth in his tracks. He rolled the globe behind his front paws. It felt good against his heart.

A scrawny and scruffy fox slipped onto the road. Not much like those aristocratic foxes in Druida City. Zanth stood as tall as this one and carried more muscle and mass.

But the last time he fought a fox his emerald stud had been ripped from his left ear and lost. He'd also teleported home with a broken hind leg.

FamMan Rand T'Ash had sworn and had taken a long time to make the new stud.

FamWoman Danith had cried.

Mine! the fox yelled again.

Zanth didn't run from fights. He could win against this dog fox. The fox lifted his lip, showing teeth, and Zanth growled back, packing it with power. The fox set his paws and hunkered, ready to fight.

Go away! Zanth commanded. *This is my place and all here belongs to ME. All prey, all leaves to chase, and essspesssially this TREASURE THING.*

The fox barked challenge. Zanth hissed and growled until he could only hear himself. Then he grinned because the fox hopped backward. Still, something showed in the animal's eyes that told Zanth the fox might pounce if he turned his back, or took his gaze off the fox to enjoy his new treasure.

Leave the sphere, said the fox.

The orb sent warmth into Zanth's middle. He wanted it. He would have it. *This Treasure Thing is Mine, Mine, Mine, Mine, Mine, Mine!* Zanth switched his tail. That was that. Six "mines" and that pointy-nosed creature should know it was his. Cats never backed down after six "mines."

The fox snapped out a bark. *That landscape globe belongs to my FamWoman. She made it.*

Zanth sniffed. *Then why doesn't she have it?*

She makes them and lost some. I have retrieved two.

Zanth saw in the fox's mind that there had been three. He reverted to the slum speech of his kittenhood. *ME HAS THIS ONE!*

Again the fox showed a lift of upper lip and muzzle, growled. This time the toughness of battle reflected in his eyes. *Del made it with sweat and blood and Flair.* A shifting of balance of the paws and tail. The stringy fox would fight.

With one strong kick of a hind leg and a demonstration of his own fabulous Flair, Zanth sent the "landscape globe" soaring back into the estate, between the rails of the green-iron gate.

The fox narrowed his eyes, flexed his dark, dirty claws.

Zanth matched glares. *I am Zanth, and the bauble is Mine. I will win.* He swaggered forward and his very presence made the fox step back.

Zanth. I have heard of Zanth, the fox said.

Of course. Zanth smiled with all his fangs. *I have killed many sewer rats, many celtaroons, sired many litters.*

With a long stare, the fox looked Zanth from tooth to tail tip. *You are uglier than I thought.*

Zanth curled his lip. *You are so ugly the twinmoons hide.* They'd gone behind a cloud.

You are FamCat to T'Ash, the fox stated.

It was a rare fox who could match insult with insult and this one obviously wasn't so smart, though annoying all the same. *T'Ash is MY FamMan.*

The fox darted in and swung a paw. Zanth hopped aside, then hissed and surged forward, back arched, all his hair out. Yes, he was more muscular, thicker than this stupid, scrawny fox.

It hunched it's back and screeched so Zanth had to flatten his ears.

I WILL fight you! Even as he rumbled a growl deep in his throat, Zanth's thoughts sped.

In a fight he might lose his emerald ear studs and his collar. FamMan refused to fix them again or make him more. FamWoman would be sad. Tears might drip down her face and onto Zanth's fur like the last time he came back bloodied. That made him feel almost worse than losing his gems.

But he extended his claws. He let battle anticipation sit on his tongue before saying, *I am Zanth and I will win this battle, as I win ALL My battles.*

He paused. He was so clever. Then he said, *But...*

The fox snapped up Zanth's bait. *What?*

I could pay you for the landscape globe with rabbit. In Zanth's experience foxes loved rabbit.

His adversary's tongue rolled out and a string of drool hung to the ground. *Real Earthan rabbit or the Celtan mocyn?* the fox asked.

Snorting, Zanth said, *Rabbits. Two. Freshly killed and put in a cold spot where I can get in with my Flair.* A neighboring farmer had done the killing, but Zanth didn't care. If it was available to him and no one guarded it from him, it was his.

Done! cried the fox, and he was equally irritating as he kept up with Zanth on the run to the neighbor's cold shed.

Feeling magnanimous, Zanth showed the creature how to manipulate the latch with Flair. The fox took both rabbits while Zanth sat and groomed his paws. The treasure was his and it would last a lot longer than a couple of rabbit meals. Besides, he didn't like rabbit.

Once they were away from the shed and the road, they eyed each other, then the fox nodded and said, *I am Shunuk.*

I haven't heard of you, Zanth said.

The fox's tail bristled and flicked, then he was gone in the night, nearly as quiet and stealthy as Zanth himself.

Zanth hurried back to his estate to claim his treasure. He stared at it and for an instant in the twinmoons' light an image solidified inside the sphere. Zanth's Residence and room and his velvet pillow. He lipped up his treasure and grinned around the globe.

He was the strongest and cleverest and best FamCat... FamAnimal...on all of Celta. Naturally.

Life was good.

=The End =

BACCAT CHOOSES HIS PERSON

There were three reasons I wanted to tell this story:

1) I wanted to show how Baccat (who appeared in Heart Secret as a nameless gray tabby) transitioned from being one of Garrett Primross' feral informers to FirstFamily GrandLady Loridana D'Yew's Fam in Heart Legacy;

2) I had trouble with Heart Legacy's opening, and before I settled on the current opening I wrote a new piece that was, again, more backstory than I needed (sometimes writers need to know backstory that doesn't appear in a book), but I liked the scene and thought it could become part of Baccat's story;

3) And, finally, I wanted to have a Yule ritual I could post on my blog and Facebook.

That last didn't happen in this story because it's difficult writing a Yule ceremony from the point of view of a cat who has little interest in it, and a detailed ritual doesn't belong in a short story unless the story is all about how that particular ritual transforms characters.

Baccat's story is about how he found his true FamWoman.

Perhaps that's too much information. Ignore it and, I hope, enjoy Baccat's story.

Also note Baccat has a larger vocabulary and more formal expression than the other cats in this collection.

424 YEARS AFTER COLONIZATION, **Druida City, Early Winter**

Not the time for a civilized, respectable, *intelligent* cat to be out. A proper cat like himself, *Baccat*, who embodied great enough attributes to become a *Familiar Companion* to a human. He needed to find a person who would put him first.

The sun had disappeared behind a bank of thick clouds before it should have set, darkening the world. Autumn had faded away with spitting sleet and winter threatened frost, and worse, snow.

His only slightly hardened pads shriveled with cold as he trotted light-footed along the cold sidewalks in the overcast night.

Currently he slept in a dirt hollow under thick bushes behind the Turquoise House, another intelligent being, though quite immobile. The House already contained two resident cats — one the small Pinky and the other the dangerous Ratkiller, and Baccat would not ask to live inside on sufferance.

Baccat sniffed in disdain, and his nose twitched. Yes, snow ladened those low clouds, ready to drift down on him at any moment and make the world around him white and cold and bleak. A big whisker-tall snow threatened.

He was cold and hungry but did not really like the taste of raw mouse, of newly killed anything. And he disliked the effort and energy and magic psi-mind power, *Flair*, he had to use to hunt.

Yes, he needed a FamMan or, better, a FamWoman. One to care for him, one who would like him *best*. One who would comb and brush his thickening gray-white fur, keep the darker gray stripes even and pretty. A human who would rub ointment into his cold-reddening-raw ears.

He'd been on the prowl for a Fam companion. Perhaps he held too high standards.

Was there such a thing as too high a standard for a human? Probably.

But none of the lower nobles near the Turquoise House seemed appropriate. None of their minds free from stupid human busymindedness to even *notice* him and his potential.

The first test of a good companion. To recognize *him* as a superior FamCat.

No one in the busy Yuletide street fairs — lower class browsers, middle-class vendors, or noble class casual buyers — had given him a second glance. It pricked his *amour propre*. Not one of them would shop for a necklace that would match his light green eyes.

No one had given him a New Year's, Samhain's, gift last month. Not even a crumpled ball of papyrus to play with like his third and least-liked professor FamMan had given him.

When the first of his three professors died more than a year ago, Baccat tried living on the streets. He'd joined the gang of Fams that the private investigator, Garrett Primross, fed.

He'd helped solve a murder before he finally returned to the other two professors who shared the small apartment provided by the college. The last one had passed on at the end of the summer, and Baccat's home had been assigned to a Person With A Dog!

Who disliked *him*. Impossible to stay.

He needed to find shelter before the winter. *Someone to put him first.*

※

TIME TO EXPAND his search for a proper human companion.

In the dim light he saw humans gathered in the park ahead. They stood away from the temple near a large firepit with one big log and a lot of smaller branches and wood. The people moved around briskly, voices raised in cheer that didn't touch Baccat's sour mood.

He'd wait and study the people before he joined their Yule ritual and spent much of the evening with them. Only three other Fams showed up with their human companions. Baccat didn't know whether that meant his prospects were good because someone would want a Fam, or if his choices were, once more, of lower quality humans.

Minutes passed as he hunkered in the bushes, in a dirt wallow that didn't smell too offensively of dog.

A movement caught his eye, unnoticed by everyone else--animal, Fam, human, inside and outside of the circle. Next to the deep shadow of a tree, nearly blended into it, stood a woman. Baccat blinked, sharpened his focus on her aura. Not a mature woman. One barely adult.

She watched as he did. Interesting.

Then, as the humans sorted themselves into a circle, some of them already standing hand-in-hand, the sheer generosity of their spirits lured him to take part in their holiday.

Perhaps, perhaps, he could find a person, or even a couple, with whom he could bond. He rather liked the look of the priest who'd worked so hard on sprucing up the park and restoring the temple....

If he didn't find a human companion he'd continue to live in the wallow...in a snowy rut. His paws and ears and muzzle would deteriorate. He might die!

No, he *would* find someone to treat him *the best.* He was determined.

So he exited the rut and spent a few minutes grooming to make himself as presentable as he could without having a regular abode. Then he strolled around the circle, discreetly sniffing at the humans. Some of the people knew each other, recognized each other as neighbors, some were strangers to all.

Welcome to all.

Baccat found two, a mated couple, that particularly radiated warmth. He stepped right up and into the circle between the man and a woman and mewed. They glanced down and moved their feet so he could sit on one each of their feet and be included in the energy of the circle.

He watched as the other Fams joined their humans. They ignored him as if he were a *feral.* The nerve of them!

Baccat kept his composure as latecomers arrived, found places in the circle and it expanded opposite them. He observed the priest and priestess dressed the altar to one side of the bonfire. Those two brought out covered platters to share during the ritual and he scented furrabeast and gravy in pastry turnovers. Smelled simply delicious. He decided it was worth being here for the food, even if he didn't find a human Fam.

He shifted now and again as cold seeped through him from his derriere on the freezing ground, only blocked by the portion of him on the feet of the couple in order to link better with them and the rest of the humans.

Finally the priest and priestess took up their places and intoned the spell words that started the ceremony. From his years with the professors, he knew the order of rituals. The man and woman, representing the Divine Couple, the Lady and Lord, went to each being and connected them into the spiritual circle, then closed it magically.

To his disgust, the humans didn't erect a weathershield spell that would keep any generated warmth in.

He should have scouted out a better group, but the highest-status humans all celebrated with their Families tonight. They wouldn't open the big, round place of worship until much later, and by that time his nose might frost over.

So as the humans sent energy around the circle and he joined in, he blasted a visual of a weathershield out along the stream. The man and woman near him squeaked and shifted their feet under him, no doubt surprised at his mental power.

The priestess laughed and sent the thought that he should be patient, and that later she and the priest *would* raise a light weathershield. Baccat barely refrained from hissing at her. He sensed that, unlike him, *she'd* spent most of the day inside, clean and fed and warm.

The couple he'd hoped to impress withdrew a little from him, and dumped him out of the circle and that...no, not *hurt*. Discouraged only. He thought they'd looked askance at him. He had to lie all the way down on the ground and put one forepaw on her shoe and drape his tail over the man's shoe to link with them and the rest of the people during this blessing part of the ceremony.

Husband squeezed wife's hand and they both thought of the blessing of her body now carrying a new child. Focused on the future of their Family with that child. No thought at all of a Fam, particularly of the Fam at their feet.

Not hurt, no. Disappointed.

In the middle of the circle, the priest lit the big log and

the flames whooshed up. He threw off his mask of an older man and cloak of green and danced with the priestess. Then she helped him don a new cape of red and a holographic mask of a baby growing to a newly-adult man.

The couple linked closest with Baccat ooohed and aaahed and thought of their babe.

The priestess said human mental-magic-Words that rang within and without Baccat's ears forming a basic weathershield along with a magical dome that kept the energy inside and swirling. He remained cold and, after sending his mind around the circle considering each person and finding no one interested in him...a little sad.

Soon the people sang and swayed, then took torches from the priest and priestesses and sang about the end of the dark and welcoming light and lit their torches at the big log, then danced, waving the torches. Baccat kept a wary eye out for sparks and flying cinders, but at least the people's movement generated some heat.

When the action ended and meditation began, he returned to his original place, though had no illusions that he'd find a FamWoman or FamMan or FamCouple here. The slightly thawed ground now dampened his rump and paws and tail. Nasty.

Priest and Priestess heated the turnovers and readied the prized citrus juice drink, said more magical Words and spiritual blessings and sent the platters of hand pies and goblets around the circle.

Baccat's mouth watered but the humans did not share even a tiniest shred of furrabeast with him. Passed over just as if he were of no account. He growled but his neighbors paid no attention. The great light that seemed to have entered his chest during the climax of the ceremony, the brightness and the sparkle, faded at this lack of courtesy.

Then the priest came to him with a small portion on a piece of bark and placed it before Baccat. He thrashed his tail. *Thank you.* He paused, eying the man. He might be an acceptable person. The temple might be too cold, but the priest wore good clothing and smelled of expensive soap and spells, so he must live in a good, warm place.

Giving a tiny mew, and looking his most charming, he sent mind-to-mind to the religious man, *Would you like a Fam?* Baccat opened his eyes wide since humans liked that.

Not at all, thanks, said the man absent-mindedly and scratched Baccat between the ears, then went down the circle to another Fam and did the same!

Then the man and the woman on either side of him moved and he felt toes of shoes slide under his hindquarters to link him with everyone again. And the big, beautiful feeling in his heart came back as everyone, more cheerful than he, linked and dragged him into the emotion. He even forgot the coolness and wet of his derriere.

Finally the priest said the closing prayer and opened the circle, and vanished the weathershield and Baccat's whiskers twitched at the frigid cold. Icy breezes ruffled his hair to reach his tender skin and sink winter into his bones.

Those who *could* teleport away to their bright and warm homes, did. Most of the others, including the couple who gave him not a glance, hurried away, walking fast.

The priestess left, and the priest gestured to the stragglers — all single persons — toward the temple.

Baccat's hopes had plummeted, and he began to trudge back toward the ditch at the Turquoise House when he saw the young woman he'd noted earlier step away from the tree. She moved easily, and narrowing his eyes, he perceived that a magnificent weathershield formed around her. The fat snowflakes falling met her shield and melted, the wind swirled away from her, did not touch her.

Something about a tall, slender girl with light hair that shone in the twinmoonslight attracted him. Her scent teased him. *Animals — beloved animals marking their person.* Mostly stridebeasts. His nose twitched as he tapped a paw in counting rhythm. Eight. But one stridebeast was much like another, hardly distinguishable or unique. And they didn't live *inside* with their person. Like a FamCat would. Sleeping in her bedroom on a fancy pillow.

Since other fur-bearers, even stridebeasts, loved her, Baccat paused and considered. The girl might have possibilities.

So just as she stepped from the edge of the park into a rarely used side street, he ran across her path, moving so he'd only be a blur to her eyes.

His resolve had stiffened. The girl had to pass his first test. He leapt onto an empty cart, waved his gray and black striped tail to attract her attention, looked over his back and met her gaze.

FamCat, she said into his mind. Nice and clear in *words,* not only a Cat image.

As he formed a reply, her expression sharpened into anxiety. She whirled around, *felt* lost.

You are near the park, he sent her.

I teleported near a plaque! Where is it? I need to know! Why am I asking a CAT?

Baccat sniffed, stalked to a small area surrounded by crates. *Here.*

A small cry escaped her. She hurried over to touch the plaque, stared around as if to fix the location in her brain.

Baccat sat tall, expecting thanks.

But she vanished, teleporting away without a sound, without leaving a wavy aura around her.

She'd passed his test, *saw* him, *acknowledged* him.

But slipped through his paws. Discouraging.

And who was she?

&.

THE NEXT NIGHT, late, after he'd devoured a few scraps from the food carts in CityCenter, he started back toward the Turquoise House. As he trotted through his usual alleys magically cleared of the big snow, Baccat caught the scent of the young woman again. His ears angled as he heard her pattering footsteps, quick and hurried, feet shod with good and well treated furrabeast leather soles.

Yesss, the same young woman as before, just past child-hood. An adult as the humans figured things.

She might be an acceptable FamWoman for him, espe-cially if her home was as rich. She wore expensive boots and clothing. He noted her skin smelled exquisitely of the finest lotions.

Pad, pad, pad, a little closer. Her breathing came fast and she appeared quite out of place. As much as he, perhaps. He'd spent his kittenhood and young adult cathood with a professor. Who'd died and made no provisions for his Fam! Dreadful.

Infuriating.

But Baccat would not dwell on that, on how low he'd fallen.

Baccat wanted the best and he thought this girl could give him that.

So, when she glanced over her shoulder to check the entrance of the alley — a large rat had scurried away from him — Baccat plunked himself down directly into her path and offered a smile, along with the words broadcast locally and telepathically, *Greetyou, Lady.*

She gasped and jumped, stumbled back with a hand pressed between her breasts.

Baccat decided not to take offense.

Apparently examining him from eartuft to tail tip, she kept silent for a moment. He'd groomed most particularly for this eventuality, working with tooth and claw to remove the mats that he could reach from his fur. Alas, since his stomach had shrunk, he could access more portions of his body. He sniffed again. She didn't smell as if she carried food. Too bad. He let a quiet exhalation sift from his mouth.

She still didn't speak and he couldn't prevent the irritation that caused his tail to twitch. *GREETYOU, LADY!* he shouted mentally, since she hadn't responded to his original courtesy.

She winced. "I heard you the first time." She said a Word and a lightspell formed overhead. Her expression turned dubious, so Baccat sniffed loudly to show he, too, considered her. When she didn't respond appropriately, he lifted his leg and began to groom.

"Oh," she said. "The FamCat from last night. You're an intelligent Familiar animal? To whom are you the companion?"

He approved of her grammar, so he lowered his leg and sat again. Now he could sense the interest and...dare he think it?...hope radiating from her. He caught the thought that she didn't think Fams would haunt alleyways in City-Center. How little did she know. CityCenter offered prime amusements for Cats. He could, perhaps, educate her when they became FamCat and FamWoman.

I am currently interviewing humans for the honor of becoming My Fam.

She snorted and he thought she might also be laughing. Laughing at *him!* Intolerable.

Pausing, she looked beyond him, stilled.

Well, if it ain't the newbie Cat to the band. The stuck-up, bottom of the clowder Cat, looking for a HUMAN to take care'a him, sneered the alpha of the feral band with whom Baccat associated.

Baccat whirled, found a semi-circle of five cats staring at them, the big black one flicking his tail in obvious challenge. Well, he matched that one in size, bested him in intelligence.

Nothing wrong with having a human feed good stuff, give good pets, said the long-haired female calico. She waved her fluffy orange and black and white tail back and forth, then rumbled a loud purr that filled the alley. *Perhaps the girl would like ME better.*

The young woman frowned, but said, "Perhaps."

Many humans good for many meals, added a black cat with white paws on a loud belch. *I could be a FamCat, too.*

Baccat's nose caught the odor of slightly off porcine strip. His stomach grumbled, he hadn't pushed to the front of the band close enough to get a few of the fresh fish guts for the evening meal, but only kibble. Not that he liked fish innards.

A chuckle from the young woman.

No use for it, Baccat must prove his worth. So much for *his* tests. She'd decided to have some of her own. Irritation mixed with approval within Baccat.

He hissed at the group. *She is MINE,* he sent along a private cat channel.

Big Black, snorted, swaggered close.

Baccat nerved himself for great use of energy and *teleported* right in front of Big Black who reared back in surprise. *YOU can't do that. Can't teleport.*

Sure I can! Big Black, a very simple name used by a very simple cat, blustered.

Let's see you do so, then! Baccat challenged. He swept his gaze along the other Cats, prodding them to echo him. And, disloyal band that they were, they did.

Yeah, White Paws stopped licking a forepaw, focused. *Let's see you, Big Black.*

Yes, the calico whispered the word, mewed aloud at the same time.

The others agreed and the woman waited.

Too cold right now, using My Flair to keep Us ALL warm, Big Black said, sending out the puny weathershield he could control to cover the rest of his band. An alpha cat trick Baccat hadn't managed to learn yet, since he spent most of his time alone. Or with humans who would shield him.

True, You shield Us, Big Black, stated calico. She smiled winningly at the FamWoman. *You might prefer a female FamCat.*

So Baccat hopped in front of *her. She might like a long-haired Cat who vomits hairballs quite often. A Cat to clean up after!*

"Oh," the woman said faintly.

And, as if he'd prompted the action, the calico began to hack.

Not Big Black or calico, but Me! insisted White Paws.

So Baccat jumped in front of him. He flinched but didn't, quite, fall. *You, White Paws, can't be loyal to one person, one human. You wander the whole town for multiple meals from multiple people.*

White Paws glanced aside.

"Loyalty is absolutely necessary," the young woman said.

And You are all more in the clowder than Me! Baccat leapt, and used Flair and did more little teleporting hops, and zoomed around them. The cats scattered, Big Black trotting, not running, as if pretending he didn't retreat.

Baccat grinned up at the woman in satisfaction. *Greetyou, GentleLady.* He inclined his head like humans did. *I am called Baccat.*

She blinked, stooped down and rubbed his head. "This is...lucky, I suppose. Perhaps an omen. *Baccat* could be a Yew—, a derivative of my Family name."

A minor member of the Huckleberry Family named Me, Baccat said. Since she'd looked up at a faint rat chittering, then straightened, he decided against telling his story to her at this moment.

Mind-to-mind, she sent, *You can call me Lori. I am NOT a girl. I am an adult as of last summer.* Then she cleared her throat and said aloud, "I'd planned on, ah, looking at City-Center, but the energy of the Yule ritual drew me to the park to watch." She glanced around and he followed her gaze. The distant park behind them showed absolutely no one. Before them the alley narrowed and branched into even smaller twisty byways.

You have wandered far from CityCenter, he stated. More like a PublicCarrier ride than a walk, especially on a freezing winter's night.

Just followed some of the back streets, she replied.

I know where We are, and where We are in conjunction to CityCenter. If you hold Me, I can take Us there, he offered. It would demand a great deal of his Flair to teleport them both there. He'd expended much magic tonight, but he'd soaked up some energy and power from the ritual. And he needed to impress this woman who would give him a nice home.

She picked him up and now, so close, he smelled a trace of tangy not-natural stuff. He sniffed discreetly. *You have an odd scent on your clothes.*

Her bosom jerked and a choked laugh expelled from her.

"I am restoring the boathouse," she said, stiffening a little as if in defense. "The *Family* thinks I am working on a stall or two of the stables, which I did three months ago. I make it a policy to always be ahead of my assigned projects."

Thus you have time to explore Druida. Baccat revved his purr louder.

"Ye-es." Then she switched to mental communication with him. *I first left my est—the Family place— just two days ago. I am unsure about staying—* The telepathic phrases, freighted with emotions of disappointment and dread, collapsed into muddy images, then wide and deepening hurt.

He radiated warmth, sent comfort — the comfort he'd received from her and returned, along with the true plea-sure of being with her. His brain calculated, though. Now he lay against her bosom and could definitely feel the wealth of her Flair, her magical power, he knew it to be the strongest he'd ever sensed. From anyone.

Being within her weathershield kept him toasty and warm, and even the passive Flair radiating from her sank into him. *Wonderful!*

He thought swiftly. He'd caught fragmented images, the slip of her mind-images. She'd nearly said *estate* and her mind had shown a mansion and a great amount of land *in Noble Country,* where the highest status and richest people lived. Also, she'd emphasized *Family*, as if she capitalized the first letter, which meant a noble Family.

She had the strongest power. She'd treat him the best.

You wanted to see Druida CityCenter? he said.

Yes, please, Baccat, she replied precisely, but her thoughts blurred as if she hid any specific goal from him.

So he bent his mind for precise images of the broad street opposite and perpendicular to the GuildHall, to a small business teleportation alcove there. He checked the pad and no light showed it was in use.

Humans count down for teleportation. I shall not do that, so prepare yourself. He gathered his Flair, and a little from her, calculated her height so they'd land well.

"Wait—" she began.

But he moved them through space in an instant and they lit without any jolt. Well done. Impressive. He grinned around his whiskers.

"Oh!" Her breath huffed out and her hold loosened and Baccat discovered some of his fur stuck to her palms. She'd perspired. Slightly disgusting. He leapt from her clasp to outside her weathershield which had also heated uncomfortably. She might be an adult, but as far as he could determine, she didn't have complete control of all that massive Flair within her.

This way. He exited the teleportation pad alcove and loped to the boulevard circling CityCenter. Nothing moved on streets or sidewalks this late winter holiday night. He glanced over his shoulder to see her coming, then sat on the elegant but frigid flagstones of the sidewalk, and indicated buildings with his paw. *Before us is the new GuildHall, on the curve to the left is the Main Druida City Guardhouse and the official offices of the Botanist's, Jeweler's, and Transport Guilds. On the curve to the right are retail shops.*

"Does the GuildHall, ah, contain archives?" she asked, then shook her head, murmured, "As if a *cat* would know."

Of course I know. Baccat emphasized his words with a disdainful sniff. *I lived with the professors, Huckleberry, Cantaloupe, and Sievabean for all of my life.* He let the weariness mixed with a touch of sadness that filled him again at the memories of his pleasant childhood lace his next words. *For the last of their lives, too. They have moved on to the Wheel of Stars.* A polite way of saying they died.

"Oh!" Lori reached down and petted him and he leaned against her trous and purred, making sure he rubbed her legs and marked the fabric with *his* scent should those *other* cats sneak and lurk close again.

He displayed his knowledge in precise tones. *The Clerk of the GuildHall records events and items like the maps of the geography of Celta, and holds the official records of all the Guilds of Celta.* He slid his gaze to meet hers, answered what he thought she wanted to know. *All the records of the Noble Councils are kept there, too.* Another rub against her leg. *From the very first, after the colonists landed on Celta.*

A quick intake of air from her. "Even the FirstFamily Councils?" She paused slightly and back-ruffled his hair, then smoothed it down. Not a petting procedure he liked.

Even the FirstFamilies Council. He thought hard, straining his memory. *Up to the last and latest.* He left it at that, since he didn't really know when the latest and last would have been.

A whiff of yearning flickered from her, and he smelled change in her body from anticipation, but also *emotion.* Which meant they had formed a link between them. Excellent.

He crooked his tail. *I am not sure if GuildHall is open now or if there is a clerk on duty.* The flagstones under his paws did not warm much and the cold began to make them ache. *I suspect that if You did look at the archives this night after Yule, you would be remembered.*

She shivered, more with anxiety than a chill, he sensed.

"What...what of a...library?" Her brows came down. "I think something is open to everyone?"

The PublicLibrary. He gave her the right word for her concept. He undulated his tail to catch her attention and show his pleasure at being with her. He'd noticed human expressions softened to dogs when they thrashed their tails around in such a manner. But he hid his dismay.

The PublicLibrary, just one street down, had FamCats. Two. Who disliked him, wouldn't let him inside or even loiter a little on the grounds. Terrible, snotty, snobs.

The PublicLibrary is across the circle and down a half-block. The library will be open, but it is a sentient building like a First-Families Noble Residence House—

"I know about intelligent buildings. The Library will note who comes in on a very quiet night just after Yule, too."

"Yesss," Baccat vocalized.

At that moment, the large doors of the Guardhouse popped open and two guards, a male and female, exited the building.

Coming off shift, Baccat murmured to Lori. The guards strode the opposite direction, but more marching steps broke the silence. He and Lori turned, a little too late to avoid the guardsmen.

The guardsmen paused to study them.

They might remember You, too, Baccat sent to the young woman's mind, knowing she didn't want that.

My weathershield blurs my face a little, she said, but he heard the uncertain note in her voice.

That is a good trick, he approved, and as he watched the

weathershield strengthen. Yes, her features blurred, becoming less refined. Definitely a noble.

"A girl!" exclaimed an older guard.

"What do we have here?" The younger man, surely not much older than Lori, asked.

"Not a good night to be out," the older one grunted, brows dipping. "Can we escort you home?"

"I, ah, no—"

No use for it. Baccat hopped up and down to attract their attention. *An adult woman. And I am with her. I will defend her.*

"Cat bodyguard," the younger one snorted, then narrowed his eyes and rudely pointed at Baccat. "Hey, I know you. You're one of the feral toms who works with the private investigator, Jer—, Gar—"

"Garrett Primross," the older man ended.

"Yesss," Baccat said aloud again, then sent to their minds. *The clowder who work with Primross are observers and bodyguards.* He stood straight, lifted a forepaw and flexed his claws. *I can defend her.* Even though he hated fighting.

"Pretty damn big cat," the younger guard said.

Bells began to ring throughout the city, marking a new day.

"Gotta get to work," the older guard said. "You two take care, and go directly home, now."

"We will," Lori agreed breathlessly in a higher voice. She picked Baccat up.

With two last hard glances, the guards marched off to the station.

❧

SHE HELD him as she hurried back to the teleportation pad alcove.

They do not watch, Baccat informed her. He purred outrageously to make her feel good. Then a second of *darkness* as she teleported them away from the alley and to a different empty courtyard of flagstones surrounded on three sides by low buildings, only one and a half of which appeared in good shape.

One whiff on his in-caught breath told him they landed in a stables area. He turned at snuffling noises, and saw a couple of stridebeasts looking out the top half of doors. Baccat fluffed his fur a bit to keep his own warmth in at the sight.

"I don't know," Lori said aloud. Doubt pulsed from her. "Perhaps you should stay here in the stables with the stridebeasts. It will be safer."

He rotated his ears in offense, but he kept that emotion from radiating to the girl, didn't even let his muscles stiffen in insult. Baccat had smelled a *Residence*, an old, old intelligent house that only the best of the best, the richest of the rich had.

He wanted *in.*

I would rather come with You. Desperate measures called for, he turned and licked her cheek.

But she continued to the door of the block that housed the stridebeasts, then went down the stalls, greeting them with light touches of her mind and affection that also flowed over Baccat.

She showed him an open door of a clean stall. As he stared at the bedding, a blanket — smelling of stridebeasts — floated down. "This would be a good place for you." For some reason, her voice lowered. "My Family is...not...generous of spirit." Now her tone turned wistful. "Our Yule 'celebration' was nothing like the one I observed in the park. Nothing that kind or sharing."

Families are often harder to deal with in a ritual circle than strangers, I have heard. He'd paid little mind to his Professors grumblings about Families, but they'd done it enough the sentiments had sunk in.

"I always thought Families were supposed to be *more* loving than strangers," she said, then nibbled her lip. "At least I believe I read that."

Baccat snorted. *Families are what they are.*

"And mine is not nice, more like mean. I think it best if you stay here."

He'd suffered plenty of petty meanness with three aging academic bachelors.

He sent her much, much, love, purred and murmured telepathically. *I will be fine. We will be fine, FamWoman.*

"FamWoman," she breathed, glanced down the stalls and again he felt her lonely heart. "Someone who will reply when I talk to him. A FamCat. *My* FamCat."

Yes, FamWoman. Let Us go into the Residence and bond better. In a deliberately hesitant voice, he asked, *Don't I belong inside with You?*

She squeezed him tighter. "Yes."

I belong with My FamWoman. Inside with My FamWoman.

On her bed.

"GET HIM! GET THE NASTY CAT!" a woman's voice shrieked, yanking Baccat from a catnap that had deepened into foggy sleep. Surely he hadn't been asleep long. Hard to think.

The burst of full light in the bedroom blinded him.

"I'll kill him!" a man gloated.

That sent fear through Baccat's every nerve. He tried to

breathe deeply but stuff stopped up his nose. He opened his mouth, curled his tongue, tasted...sweat of evil beings.

"No, cousins!" Lori jerked up beside Baccat. "No, Vi! No Zus!" Her voice sounded weak, too. Baccat could hear the rapid pumping of her heart. Her fingers twitched as she reached for him just on the next pillow, but didn't move more than a couple of centimeters.

Uh-oh.

He contemplated his paws under him, raised to them, fell over as paws — and eyes — crossed. His tongue protruded from his muzzle.

This was bad.

"Stop!" whispered Lori, then sent a thought to Baccat, *Gas! We've been gassed and drugged.*

Bad! He could not sweat, and if he panted, he might take more of the drug in. These people appeared much like Lori's, no more than two years older than she. Cousins, she'd said. Yes. Alike, brother and sister, twins. With faces contorted in vicious expressions. Weak chins... greedy eyes.

Baccat had been in bad spots before, seen death on human faces coming to him before.

Lori tried to roll toward him, defend him? Got tangled in the sheets.

"I'll take care of him." Zus, the male, moved quicker now.

"You know the rules we live by, puny little girl!" Vi shrilled. Pointing a finger at Baccat, Vi continued, "No animals inside. Our Residence doesn't like them!"

Inconceivable that a Residence would dislike a Fam. Baccat's mind scrambled. His brain sent urgent alarm throughout him. *Move!*

"He's not a cat he's an intelligent animal companion, a Fam!" Lori's voice yet sounded whispery, but intense.

Vi snorted. "You lie."

"I don't, and the Residence, who monitors me, knows I don't! Residence, I want my Fam!" Lori demanded. "Surely you've had Fams before."

"It's been a very long time," the Residence answered querulously.

"But Familiar animal companions are important and should be treated like members of the Family," Lori insisted.

Baccat lay dredging energy and Flair from the very cells of his body. To move. To survive.

"I do not like the small mobile animal inside my walls. Not at all."

"Best to just get rid of it." Zus smiled with glee in his eyes. A smack against his palm signaled that he'd translocated a knife. It gleamed nastily in the bright light flooding the bedroom.

"No!" Lori flung off the covers, surged toward Zus.

Moving too slowly.

As was Baccat. But he gathered himself. Soon, soon.... He *would NOT die now he found a good FamWoman.*

The man sheathed the knife, smiled with glee in his eyes. "We'll take care of you first, leave more time to have fun with the cat." He snapped his fingers and opened his hand and dull and ugly cuffs lit there, translocated from somewhere else.

"Get her! Hold her!" he snarled at the woman who looked too much like him, down to the nasty expressions on their faces. The woman, Vi, lunged at Lori and missed, Lori side-stepping agilely, Vi trundling around, *not* graceful for all her slenderness.

But the bad man cuz, Zus, did a short teleporting hop, grabbed Lori's arm, hard enough that bruises bloomed, and snapped one cuff on her.

Immediately the bright glow of her Flair magic power

dimmed.

All Baccat's fur raised straight up at the sight! The cuffs stopped her from using her magic. *Depress Flair bracelets.* Terrible! He'd only seen such evil things in the university museum.

Fury poured through him, finally, finally, energizing him.

His Lori had done *nothing* to merit this.

With a yowl he forgot he hated fighting. That fighting someone larger always brought pain. He Flair-leapt at Zus and Lori, caught claws in the shirt covering the man's upper chest, ripped at silkeen cloth and human skin. Matched Zus' pained shriek with Baccat's own battle yowl.

Red runnels showed through sliced shirt. Baccat freed his claws, gaged his next move, hopped lightly to Lori's up flung arm and hit just right! Hit the lock of the cuff and broke the innards with *his* Flair power.

"Get the cat, Residence! Find him with inner wind! KILL HIM!" Zus ordered.

The room creaked around them.

Pale white and panting, Lori grabbed Baccat. He curled into her, making himself smaller, and she *teleported them away.*

Once more they lit in the middle of the stable courtyard. This time the door to the main stable block wrenched open — Lori's Flair — and they strode through it into the dimness of stalls, the clean smell of fresh straw and the radiating love of the animals.

She loosened her grasp and Baccat leapt to a wooden bench and stared at her. Her whole body trembled with suppressed anger and Flair. He saw the emotions but didn't *feel* them. No, she penned them up inside her so as not to scare her animals.

Remarkable.

She looked at him with a strained expression. "You have seen my Family. You will never be allowed in the Residence, even as my FamCat. If you wish to remain my FamCat. Do you? Do you stay here with me or go?" she asked tightly.

He made his eyes big and round. Saw the flash of pain in hers. As if she thought he'd go.

That she acknowledged the choice was his, pleased him. And she needed him. Needed him more than anyone had in his whole life. More than his old, best professor who only threw him scraps and thought of him as a *pet*.

Stay or go? Her telepathic voice sounded cool, but she held herself stiffly, and he felt hurt behind.

Her nasty Family had hurt her, and she had no one to sympathize. No intelligent friends, animals or humans.

He felt a little small.

He would not be of the highest class of Cats. Despite her title as the leader of a FirstFamily, she did not hold the true power.

But he'd be loved. He could feel that huge warmth in her generous heart. He'd be a true Fam Companion, as he realized he'd never been.

She loved him like no other human had. Would bond with him as no one else had.

Even if he slept in stables smelling of stridebeasts and ate scraps instead of sleeping on a pillow in a Residence and munching the finest furrabeast, the bond between himself and Lori surged and flowed with love.

Love was better than status.

Stay, he said, and stretched out to lick her hand.

= The End =

ZANTH SAVES THE DAY

Dedication: To Shawna Lanne, my Facebook friend, for her help in brainstorming this story. Thanks!

I wrote this story as part of promotion for the Coastal Magic Convention of February, 2018, then I decided I wanted another Zanth story in this collection...so I'll have to write another for Coastal Magic.

BEACH OF T'ASH's New Southern Estate, Celta, 424 Years After Colonization, Summer

"Help me!" A teeny, tiny voice struck FamCat Zanth's sharp ears in an accented language of Familiar companions. He twitched and rolled over in the deep bed of sweet-smelling beach herb.

"Help me!"

"I'm lost!" whimpered an even higher voice. It echoed in Zanth's mind as much as his ears.

He wished his FamWoman Danith hadn't cleaned his ears the night before. She'd removed the sand from his first explorations of the beach yesterday, and a lot of old wax, too.

Two more new voices sounded against the background of "Help," and "I'm lost."

"I must get to the ocean," cried the third voice.

"The ocean! It will save and feed," squeaked a fourth.

A short pause of silence and Zanth breathed in the fine scent of summer and sand, stretched a little in the nice heat of the sun.

Then *all* of the little beings screeched at once, both aloud and mentally, "*I am scared, I am scared, I am scared, I am scared...*"

He couldn't sleep through that. Opening an eye, he looked around, saw nothing.

The chant, and the feeling of fear, increased in nasty uncomfortable waves making him ruffle his black-and-white fur, rise to his paws, look around. He saw sand and sea oats and grasses and bushes and his patch of herb. In the distance rolled the big gray water, threatening. It had crept up more of the beach than felt comfortable.

Some sand fell off him and he shook himself, making sure the sand didn't dust his black fur or dim his white parts. He whipped his black tail to flick granules away. Swept one of his white forepaws over his whiskers, removing stuff, slurped up a last sticky herb leaf.

Salt rimmed his nostrils and snapped to lay on his tongue when he opened his mouth to use his smell-taste sense.

A strange tang in the air that hadn't been there a few minutes ago.

He sniffed. Smelled broken egg, but not from clucker. Some nasty liquid drying in the sun.

Heard little scratching scrabbles.

Padding softly through the warm sand, he followed his nose, saw a hole in the sand twice the size of his curled self and deep enough that he could stand on all fours and just look over the rim.

And if he jumped down and waited, the awful, encroaching water could get him. All his fur raised at the thought.

"Eeek, big scary shadow!" screeched a voice so high it pierced Zanth's mind.

Inside the hole roiled a mass of little beings crawling over shell shards, appearing a bit more slimy than he cared to touch. Lifting his upper lip of his muzzle, he looked at them with a disapproving eye. Very ugly things.

Mostly shell, maybe even too tough to eat already.

"Heellllppp!" the things chorused, moving the limbs sticking out from their body shells awkwardly.

And as the words echoed in his mind, his stomach squeezed in revulsion. Bad taste in his mouth, a tickle at the bottom of his throat like he'd vomit. Which meant he couldn't eat them because they were sentient FamAnimals. Or could be FamAnimals if they grew more.

They'd always be ugly, though.

"Look, a Big Thing!" one squealed. *Big green eyes watching us.*

No SHELL! shrilled another, shocked.

NO SHELL, the others echoed.

Dark and light weedy stuff on his body!

All of their little heads craned toward him, shiny beady eyes fixed on him.

He smelled that they were all little females.

Urgh.

"Will it help?" asked one, even as others scrabbled under their sisters.

He counted them. Two paws worth of claws. What people called *ten*.

A couple tried crawling up the hole, but the sand gave way and they tumbled back down. Hole might have been a slight indentation when their eggs were first buried, but nature or animals or something had dug it deeper and the babies were stuck.

That hadn't seemed to occur to them, yet. But Zanth understood their problem.

He'd have liked to have turned his back on them and abandoned them to their fate, but he couldn't stay on the beach while they died. Would make him uncomfortable. And maybe sad.

He had begun to love the beach, the smells and the endless soothing sound of the waves coming and going. He'd like to stay and nap.

He considered. If he saved them, he could be a hero. Again. He liked being a hero, the extra good furrabeast steak, the additional pats and pets, the praise and smiling expression FamWoman gave him for days and days.

FamMan might even make Zanth a new earring. He'd had his eye on a yellow diamond that FamMan had selfishly refused to give him.

Yes, he'd be a hero.

He dipped his head into the hole. "*Greetyou, young creatures. What are you?*" He thought he knew, he'd seen a couple of beings that looked like them on his FamMan's land.

"We are tutts..."

"Turts..."

"Tulles..."

"Turtles!" One finally got it out right.

"*We are sea turtles!*" They all chorused in his mind, definite now.

You smart animals, Zanth informed them telepathically. *Since you can talk, and talk mind to mind with Me. *I* am FamCat. THE FamCat of Celta,* he ended grandly, revealing the highest of his high status.

Ooooh! the little female turtles cooed in his mind while making odd clicking sounds, maybe their beaks. Zanth didn't know. Didn't much care.

But we can't SEE the ocean. We must go there. Now! one insisted. She had climbed on top of her sisters and stretched her neck to look at Zanth.

Yep, their smarts sizzled through their brains. Their tiny brains. Amazing they could think a-tall.

You in hole. Think you should not be. Who knows?

I don't know, someone said.

Not me, said another.

Zanth closed his eyes. *That was not a question to answer.*

He heard baby turtle sounds and they all seemed to be moving again, trying to get out of their hole. Looking down at it with distaste, he figured that he'd have to get down there and lift the little ones up.

Or dig a ramp. That would take long and his white paws would get all gritty and when he groomed he'd have to spit out sand... Easier to just jump in.

But bottom of hole looked ick. And maybe the shells would cut his paws.

Huffing a breath, he figured that this hero business tried a good FamCat.

He moderated his cat sounds so they would vibrate right in the Fam language. "All move toward sun, clear space for Me. Get you out of hole, you head for water...ocean," he corrected.

Yesssss! They sounded thrilled. More joyous clickings and their legs moved faster until they almost scuttled.

Zanth lowered his hind right leg into the hole, tipped and slid into it, thankfully squashing no one.

But a sharp shell shard poked his butt. He swatted it away. Other bits, and sand, stuck to his fur. Nasty.

I meant to do that, he sent mind-to-mind.

One of the turtles crawled over his paw. *I am ready for mother ocean, let me go!*

No use for it, he had to close his mouth around her. Just as he thought, didn't taste good. He put her over the lip of the hole, nudged her in the direction of the big and restless water.

Her back legs moved, sending a tiny spray of sand into his eyes. He grunted, bent, picked up another awful tasting thing, this one with grit attached to her, put her on the sand. Again and again.

Then a bird screeched, dove.

Toward Zanth's turtles! He flung back his head and sang his battle cry! *Pushed* with his mind to the sky and the bird.

It jerked mid-air, tumbled, barely pulled out of the steep dive and wheeled away, screeching. Other gathering birds scattered to avoid it. Then they shot away over the water, screaming bird insults at Zanth that echoed through the blue sky.

Watching his paws so he didn't step on anyone, he leapt, using a little Flair, psi power, to the top of the hole.

The first sea turtle scuffed along the sand, legs paddling madly, a whole meter away from the hole. He snorted. He'd have to help that way, too, carry them close to the white foam. Maybe he could accept slightly damp paws, but *not* wet ones. Such sacrifices he made to be a hero!

Birds still flew over the waves, watching. Waiting to see if Zanth would be less vigilant.

Little trails marked the progress of those turtles he'd

already saved.

Easy to see and find.

After a huff of breath, he hopped back into the hole and quickly lifted the other females out, then licked his fur of sea spray, to rid himself of the nasty taste. He trotted over to his herb bed to munch a bite or two so his mouth would actually feel *good* and to rest a bit before continuing his hero deeds.

Just as he considered returning to nudge them to the beginning of the wet part of the sand, he heard yells and sifting thuds in the distance.

The smell of *boy* smacked him. He lifted his head and saw them—three, carrying sharply pointed sticks—top the dunes and race through the sea oats, smashing the plants aside. Kicking and scuffing their feet, sand and uprooted plants following them down the slide of the dune.

Birds cawed raucously, still there, still watching. This time yelling more at the boys.

They waved their sticks, continuing to shout. "They've hatched and they got outta the hole we put their eggs in. Get 'em!"

Rushing toward him thoughtlessly, not even *noticing* Zanth.

The boys would run right over him, and squash his herb patch on the way to the turtles,

Zanth didn't think there'd be enough flesh on the baby turtles to make even an appetizer for one of these boys.

So they killed just for the fun of it.

He growled. *This was His Beach. He would NOT let mean boys do death to those he'd gone to great effort to save. He would NOT let them think they could intimidate HIM. Come on HIS property and do whatever they liked.*

Eying them, he jump-teleported with his mind-magic,

his *Flair*, to three meters in front of them. Bristled and showed fangs.

Me Zanth! he yelled. *You on Me's beach. GO AWAY!*

"A cat!" The biggest boy grinned at him, showing his punier human teeth, and cruelty lit his eyes.

Another boy skidded to a halt, windmilled, dropped his stick. "A *FamCat*. I dunno about this."

"Coward," the big one sneered, slapping his stick in his palm, moving his feet like he planned on attacking Zanth.

"Maybe I am a coward, but I heard a rich noble bought this land, and I'm not crossing him. I got my future to think about."

Smart boy! Zanth projected, but didn't take his locked gaze away from the big bully boy. Then he yelled proudly, *I am GreatLord T'Ash's Fam, ZANTH. Everyone knows Me!*

"I've hearda T'Ash, and I'm out. Little sport in killing baby turtles, 'specially not now." With a grunt, and a loud pop, the second boy vanished, teleporting away.

Zanth took that instant to check mentally on the little female turtles. Still on the beach near the hole. Meters and meters away from the big water.

"Whatabout you, Agal? You desertin' me?" taunted the first boy to the third.

"I dunno—" He shifted his feet back and forth, his round face slack, his eyes focused beyond Zanth on the sand and the turtles. "I like poking turtles more'n cats."

I can fight TWO. I can WIN, Zanth shouted to their dull minds. *Me BIG cat.*

"Yeah, big," the less smart boy, Agal, said. "Tall as my knees. Tough, mebbe. Might bite."

WILL BITE! Zanth confirmed. He let them see as he flexed his claws, thought about fight.

Should not kill boys, hurt them too bad. Zanth's

FamMan not like that. Hero status smudged.

First boy narrowed his eyes, rumbled low words under his breath, swung the stick. Zanth didn't flinch. Boy too far away to hit him.

Boy shot forward.

Zanth yowled his battle cry again, then, *Let's fight!*

Boy pounded the stick down, Zanth hopped left. Boy's weapon struck sand and some spit away, stinging Zanth, but boy huffed, his arm holding stick trembled.

Chest and body wide open. Zanth leapt, all claws out, hit boy, hooked claws into thin tunic, shredded it, sliced into boys skin, let himself slide down, ripping boy, to boy's crotch...

Boy screamed, dropped stick, grabbed at Zanth. He bit boy's hand, good. Teleported away and to ground. Spit out bit of boy flesh.

"*I'll kill you,*" bully shrieked.

NO YOU WON'T, Zanth shouted back. Felt full of fight and hopped around here, there, left, right, east, west.

From the corner of his eye he saw other boy look at him, at big water, at him, drop stick and run away.

Big boy lunged forward. Zanth 'ported to his shoulder, swiped claws along his forehead and blood fell into boy's eyes and he screamed and screamed.

Satisfying.

He swatted at Zanth, but Zanth had jumped down. Stood before him and jeered, *You RUN. You RUN HOME and tell ALL that ZANTH hurt you!*

The boy stumbled away.

Zanth pranced, tail waving, back to the ten little turtles, all of them scrabbling through the sand as fast as they could go. Birds had watched the fight, didn't come near, yet. But still hung around, ready to pick off babies. He flicked his tail insolently at them and they dropped their wings, but continued to circle.

He would not let them eat turtle Fams, no!

He'd won against both enemies. Won, won, *won!*

All his senses had sharpened. Big water now closer than ever, soon might reach his herb patch. No more napping in the sun.

Smell of small turtles and sand and old egg shell. Bright light of midday warming his fur, beach under his paws soft.

Life was good.

Now to be hero.

He picked the first up and trotted with her to where the sand went damp. A little too far. Put her down, went back and did it again and again and again, spitting sand out after each.

Kept track of the birds who still waited.

Finally Zanth got the remaining baby turtle, moved at an angle with her to where the others waited for them, watching the ever-creeping-closer white part of the big, gray water.

Eee! Eee! EEEeee! the last littlest female squealed.

And something bit Zanth in his right haunch.

He flinched, moved, felt muscle tear. Bending around he hissed.

At a huge turtle that had risen from the sea.

Mama! the baby in his mouth chortled.

Mama, mama, mama! they all shrilled in Zanth's mind.

Uh-oh.

Zanth opened his mouth to let the one he carried go and she dived—*Flair* magic power slowed her plunge and gently placed her in the small pool around the mother where the others paddled.

FamTurtle, Me saved your babies, he said.

The big turtle removed her beak from around his upper leg. He faced off with her, refusing to show pain.

This is not Earth. I came back to help my younglings.

Her beady gaze fixed on him.

Me saved babies! he insisted. *From birds! From boys!*

He did! He did! they cried.

I slept off the coast, heard my dearlings stir and hatch. Her head craned. *Ten eggs I laid, I have ten live hatchlings in the sea with me. Unheard of.*

Me saved. Me HERO. If he thought about the pain he would sick up herb bits and his last meal. He only had to deal with turtle. FamWoman was Animal Healer, she would mend him, but pain went through him like the encroaching and receding water.

They stared at each other. One minute. Two.

I do not like cat on my beach where I lay my eggs. Not even an intelligent cat.

MY beach.

No. She snapped her beak a millimeter away from his muzzle. He stood his ground.

I am land animal. My human FamMan land animal. OUR beach.

No—

You have ten hatchlings from ten eggs. Because Me saved. Me and FamMan and FamWoman will always save if We here, he promised.

He felt a hum from the turtle but she said nothing. The babies swam around and climbed on her, a couple moved back onto the wet sand of the beach.

More staring and his leg hurt bad. So he puffed himself up, said the magic words, *FamWoman is Danith D'Ash, THE Animal Healer of Celta.*

The mother turtle's eyes widened. The tough, old being

nodded. *Very well. You are allowed on my beach.*

Zanth sniffed. *Good.*

But I remember this beach, the smell of the sand and ocean as they come together here, the consistency of the sand and the kind of shells that make it. I remember. And I'll remember YOU, too, cat! A threat. *And so will my daughters.*

Good, Zanth replied. *They remember Me hero!*

The mother eyed him. "You may have one."

Zanth stared at her, appalled.

She glanced down at her hatchlings, looked up and scrutinized Zanth. *Even I have heard of the wonderful Danith D'Ash, the Animal Healer. You are a big cat and can hold two in your mouth. You may take two.*

No. He must have heard her wrong.

I think our meeting was meant. The words came to his mind even more ponderously, dropping like stones into his brain, bringing ripples of turtle thought-stuff he didn't want to know about.

She nosed the two smallest—of course the smallest—toward Zanth. *These two are likeliest to die in the first years. You take them.*

He sniffed. They smelled bad, worse now that sand and seaweed and stuff covered them. They mighta pissed and pooped, too, though Zanth didn't know why 'cause he hadn't seen them eat anything.

Hurry up! We don't have all day. The younglings must have food and seawater and I must take them to the continental shelf.

She was the one talking and moving so slowly.

Water lapped over his feet! Zanth hissed and hopped, then the roar and swish and swash of it changed as it hit him, turning into a burble and it *slurped.*

All the turtles laughed.

I will put them on your back. Do NOT drop them as you take them to Danith D'Ash, the Animal Healer.

Before he could protest, two little beings snuggled into his fur. He wished it was even shorter than it was.

Fare well, Zanth FamCat. You may call me with your mind, and so may your FamMan and FamWoman. I am Swift-In-The-Sea.

He doubted that, but he nodded. He wanted to teleport but his hurt leg fuzzed his mind.

Then he felt the rub of the old female's head and pain went away and his flesh mended.

He stared at her.

She did not look back, gathered her remaining hatchlings around her and disappeared into the great and nasty wet.

The last of the fight energy dribbled out of him and he decided to walk home.

He looked up at the birds who still waited. *You attack Me and the turtles on Me and you will pay with your lives.* He visualized men with blasters shooting the birds. He'd make that happen if they hurt him or turtles.

With last screechings, birds whirled away.

Zanth trudged up the animal path. At the top of the dune he looked back at the beach, saw a hint of the mother turtle beyond the white water with bubbles.

Still had a mental link with her, dammit.

Me will patrol My beach when here. Guard eggs, he sent to her.

He thought he saw a foreleg rise and flip at him.

She must be *so* grateful.

He'd saved the day, as usual. Of course.

Life was good.

= The End =

EXTRA SCENE

From Peaches Arrives On Celta

I write long. I usually went over the accepted word-count/pages specified in my publishing contracts, and so had to cut scenes. And sometimes I write scenes and get carried away with characters' backstory, what happened to them in the past, and the ins and outs of Celta, the worldbuilding.

That happened in Peaches Arrives On Celta. I had a very long scene in the conference room (after the third scene in the story), all about the newly Awakened colonists and how they chose their names, and what Families (First Families) they would become. I loved it, but, even from Peaches' point of view, and with his asides, I decided it shouldn't stay in the story.

So I decided to make an "Extra" portion of this book and put the full, long scene there, if you wished to read it.

IN THE CONFERENCE ROOM

They walked through double doors into Conference Room A. The place felt a lot nicer than any other human room on the Ship. One whole wall, longer than the small lounge, contained a window. Not opened to the view of space. Pale, patterned fabric forbidden for the Fams to claw covered the other walls.

Around the beautiful, long and thick red wood table sat ten people. Peaches only knew the Captain and Captain Lady.

Peaches had lived on the Ship his whole life, as had his FamMan. Everyone else in the large room had been *sleepers* in some sort of stupid tubes, set out from Earth itself as Colonists, about three whole sets of claws worth. The ones *Awakened* today all looked yellow from getting out of those tubes. Didn't look at all like the crew who'd lived and flown the Ship for generations.

Peaches didn't pay much attention to them. He and FamMan had been born on the Ship and cared more about the crew people like him.

You couldn't have gotten Peaches into one of the tubes. Not for all the catnip on the Ship.

These people had paid for the Ship and all the food and equipment and hired the crew.

FatherDam Chloe had slept in a tube, once. So had the new Captain and Captain Lady.

Peaches had heard that all three ships had gotten lost a long time ago and wandered many, many, *many* years, but lately FamMan had helped find a good planet for home.

Every single one of the *Awakened* stroked the big wood table. Not much wood in the Ship outside of the Great-Greensward, where trees lived. Very valuable.

These new people had asked to be Awakened *within two weeks of Landing on our new planet we named Celta.*

A second after he and FamMan and Chloe entered, a timer dinged as if noting when they'd be late. Peaches didn't like timers so much.

"What is *that?*" asked a red-headed woman with a saggy

face, pointing rudely at Peaches. "A *cat!*" she screeched and began sneezing.

"You'd better leave," FamMan murmured, waving the doors that had closed behind them back open.

FatherDam Chloe muttered, "She didn't list any allergies to animals on her medical history." Chloe sounded disapproving of the woman, on FamMan's and Peaches' side. Good.

The Captain stood, tall and strong and with his head fur cut too short. His face displayed new creases than when FatherDam had woken him up more than four paws of claws ago. Captain said, "That is a Familiar Animal Companion, an intelligent cat."

"What?" snapped the man beside the woman who'd buried her face in a cloth so only her thin head fur showed.

"As the briefing we loaded into your computers noted, things have changed over the course of the journey," the Captain said. "Including the development of intelligence in domestic pets who can now bond with people—"

"Humans," corrected the Captain Lady.

"*Get it out!*" shrieked the woman.

Peaches jumped from FamMan's shoulder and darted out the door, heard whiny woman's male mate say in a shaky voice, "Off course for two hundred years."

Trotting around to a duct that ran through the Ship, Peaches opened the grate with his *Flair*, slipped inside, then slunk back into the conference room. The Captain saw him and raised a brow, but didn't comment on his presence.

FamMan Randolph and FatherDam Chloe sat facing the window. They saw him, too. Randolph smiled, FatherDam Chloe frowned but said nothing.

Peaches padded to a spot near the window wall and

behind the older complaining woman so she couldn't see him, but he could watch the other people at the table.

He figured most of the humans wouldn't want a FamCat listening to their talk, some even discounted the smarts of the Fams, but he was there to stay. And maybe report to the other Fams, if he cared to.

Captain and Captain Lady took their seats at the head of the table. He said in a bored voice that meant he humored the other humans, "We are here at your request to discuss the new surnames we will take that will indicate our status as Founding Members of the Colonists."

Captain Lady, small and pretty with short black hair and beautiful violet eyes, slanted a narrowed glance at him and added, "Surnames that will reflect the culture we decided upon when boarding. The Celtic society the first of the founding members established on our voyage and which has been adopted by the crew."

"Of course," the peevish red-headed woman said. She sat up straight in her plush chair. "One of the reasons I, we," she patted the hand of the man next to her who only sat and watched, "requested we be *Awakened* now was to be able to choose our names first."

When no one spoke more, she continued, "Since we are here, *we* are the ones who care the most about our surnames, who particularly want one of the twelve letters of the Ogham alphabet that denote months of the year. Just think, we will have a month of the year named after *us*!"

Peaches got the idea that the woman really didn't care about a name, she just needed always to be the first to do something. He wondered if she stepped into the tubes first.

He eyed FatherDam, she appeared not to be listening, and he wondered if she would continue to fuss with the name and scold FamMan here in front of others not family. Peaches had the sinking feeling she would.

The red-head glanced down at a sheet of papyrus before her. "We have decided to choose 'Reed,' *my* birthday month."

FatherDam Chloe sat straight. "The previous Captains of this voyage, those who bought shares in the venture and worked hard to keep this Ship running, who lived and died before us, got to choose first. Some names have been taken, 'Reed' is one of them."

The woman's expression set in dissatisfied lines. Her nostrils widened.

"And of us here and awake, I think that the current Captain and his Lady should choose first." A smooth-smiling man said. Though Peaches didn't usually trust charm, he sensed the man meant well. He'd smiled at Peaches when they'd walked in.

"I don't care," muttered the Captain.

"You deserve your due," Captain Lady said, too quietly for anyone's ears except Captain and Peaches. Then she cleared her throat, "We will defer to our Executive Officer, Chloe . . . Hernandez . . . Ash. She, and her grandson, her Son'sSon, have given more service to the crew and the Ship and us than anyone living."

Uh-oh.

FATHERDAM CHLOE BLINKED. Like Captain Lady surprised her by giving Chloe first choice of names.

"Of course, the Executive Officer." Smooth guy made a little sitting bow.

"Ash, the World Tree," FatherDam Chloe murmured.

"The most important tree. The most important month that includes the Spring Equinox. Such a responsibility to live up to, such an honor to have that name. I've done well. Given good service, but . . ." Her gaze slid to FamMan as if he was lacking, though he'd proved and proved himself. Had worked hard to get a new planet. Loved her. Loved Peaches.

Peaches' fur stood up in anger at her obvious doubt.

She pressed a hand to her side, and sagged a little in her chair for a long moment while everyone looked at FamMan Randolph.

I don't like this! Peached projected to his FamMan.

Randolph's mouth tightened and he sat straight and still but redness came to his cheeks. *You were right earlier. She is more afraid than irritated at me. We can tough this out until she finds her own peace of mind again.*

Peaches hissed inside his head. He preferred fixing things.

FatherDam Chloe continued querulously. "I don't know. I'd decided decades ago, but I don't know . . ." She eyed her grandson.

"Do you want a name separate from your grandson?" pressed Woman-Who-Must-Always-Go-First.

"I like that you chose 'Ash,' a good, solid name." Captain Lady nodded.

"That was then, this is now," Chloe said.

Stupid answer. FatherDam Chloe's thinking fuzzed. Randolph looked sad before his expression blanked. Peaches hunkered down and stared at her, into her. Her anger at Peaches' FamMan, at Randolph, stirred her up again, and so soon. Not good.

"Randolph might not want Ash as a name," FatherDam Chloe tapped her fingers, slid another look at Peaches' FamMan.

Randolph angled his head. "Because I'm illegitimate?" he asked.

The Captain growled. Peaches looked at him since the Captain hadn't done that before. Not really a good Cat growl. "That should not matter." Captain hit the table with his fist. "Not with us. Not with our religion. Not—"

"Outdated Ship customs are not acceptable when we land on our new planet. There will be no concept of illegitimacy. All children are welcomed and legitimate," Captain Lady said firmly.

FatherDam Chloe shivered and frowned.

"What?" snapped the Captain.

"Just a hunch," FatherDam said, reached out and briefly touched the back of FamMan Randolph's hand. "I think you're right, all children will be . . . welcome."

Randolph inclined his head. "I'll let you decide our name, FatherDam."

A huff came from redheaded woman. Her finger touched the papyrus. "Perhaps we'll go by Beithe."

Captain Lady stared at her, eyebrows up, then leaned toward the other lady and smiled with teeth. "No. Not as a surname. You mis-remember our agreement with the colonists on the other two starships. Those who also paid for the ships and the food and the crew. We may call ourselves by the names of trees and plants from the ancient Ogham alphabet. The other founding colonists get the names of the letters."

Red-headed   Woman-Who-Must-Always-Be-First frowned, looked again at her page and opened her mouth.

The doors opened and the Pilot breezed in. "Meeting still going on?" she asked, in a voice like she'd wanted to miss it. She didn't sit down, and stood as tall as Captain, but with female curves that humans prized. For himself, Peaches liked sleek, athletic, long-backed females.

"We are choosing our surnames—" Captain Lady said.

"You're late." The Cat-hating woman sniffed. Peaches wandered under the table near her feet. She didn't cough.

All pretend. Peaches didn't like that. He moved back to where he could watch.

The Pilot raised silvery brows that matched her light-colored head fur, glanced at the woman. "*I* have duties." She smiled with sharpness. "If you want me to land this baby well." She stroked a nearby wall.

"We are discussing the names—"

"Holly," the Pilot said. "I'll take Holly. I'm single and I bought two shares in this venture, the same as you couples, so I'll remind you I get first pick. I choose Holly." With a brisk nod, she turned and left.

"Well!" huffed red-haired lady.

The older man sighed. "She had the gilt — the money — to buy two shares."

Captain went stiff.

Captain Lady leaned close to him so their bodies brushed. "*Our* money. The best investment we ever made. A new land. A new *world!*" She paused, then said, "Pilot *Holly* hid her psi powers, had a good job with a good salary in the mainstream culture."

"Not rebels like the rest of us in the ghettos for psi people," Captain ground out.

"We recognize your contribution and your leadership, Captain Bountry," repeated the smooth-talking man, his expression turned serious.

Still sounded too smooth, still *felt* sincere.

Pilot Holly is right, FamMan sent to Peaches. *This meeting is taking too long.* Randolph stood. "I ask that my grandmother, *FatherDam* for those of you who don't know our Ship slang, Chloe Hernandez, be allowed to reserve three names at this time, including Ash."

"Agreed!" Captain and Captain Lady snapped in unison.

FatherDam Chloe gasped surprise.

"That's not fair!" complained the red-headed woman.

"It leaves you with several names to choose from," Randolph said, and listed them.

Redhead sniffed again. A puny sniff that absolutely showed she had no nose problems with Peaches being near.

FamMan inclined his head to the rest of them. "I, too, have duties."

Captain grunted and stood, swept a scowl around the room. "I'd hoped to have all this set before landing." He made a cutting gesture. "Think about it, consult among yourselves. Give me a list the morning of landing. I'll announce our new Family names when we stand on Celta." He strode to the door that opened when he got near. Some of the crew lingered in the corridor and glanced in. The two guards standing beside the door, didn't. Captain nodded to the crew and said, "Upon landing, we will encourage the crew to take plant names."

I will stay and listen and watch, Peaches broadcast to FamMan and Captain and Captain Lady and FatherDam Chloe. Glancing back at those still sitting at the table the Captain ended, "Later." He walked out of the door, followed by FamMan Randolph.

"The trip lasted too long," Captain Lady said quietly, staying seated. "Our crew lost purpose and splintered into factions. We must all pull together upon landing to forge a new community. A commonality of names reflecting our new lives and culture instead our old biases on Earth is important."

The doors closed and FatherDam Chloe smiled. "The Captain is canny. Gossip will spread through the Ship and everyone will be focused on the names they want to choose."

Ash is a good name for you AND FamMan Randolph and ME, Peaches sent to her.

The smooth man looked at Peaches and smiled. "I like the name, 'Apple.'"

"Not one of the twelve months," the grumpy woman said.

"But one of the twenty-six Ogham names we are keeping for us Founders," he replied, leaning back in his chair as if ready to watch the rest of those who hadn't said anything. They looked at their own papyrus lists.

"I've made a decision," said Woman-Who-Must-Always-Be-First, sounding still irritated at the Pilot, maybe at the Captain because he left. She stood up, nose in the air. "We'll take Alder, January, the first month." Pushing back her chair, she marched toward the door.

Which didn't open automatically for her. She stopped and looked at FatherDam. Sniffed. Yes, Peaches' sniff was lots better. "I'll let you reserve your three names, Chloe, because you've contributed so much to this voyage." Her tone said she didn't think so.

Peaches shot under the table and pounced and thwapped her ankle with a soft paw. She squealed like a mouse, and jumped toward the door and it opened and she had to flop her arms around so she didn't fall down. He sniffed a *GOOD* sniff.

All around the table humans did the cough-laugh thing. Even FatherDam Chloe's expression turned more cheerful.

Standing on the threshold so the doors had to stay open

and not squish her, whiny woman gestured to her mate. "Come *on*, Henry."

He stayed sitting near the window wall. "I was second to get in the tubes behind you, Beatrice, because you wished that. *I* wanted, *want*, to see space, experience space flight. That's why I agreed to be *Awakened* two weeks out."

"Oh, you!" She flounced away and the doors closed behind her.

Everyone in the room relaxed.

Now FatherDam Chloe's mood had improved, Peaches thought about reminding her how good FamMan was.

But the mate of the woman who left turned his chair and nodded to the wall previously behind him. "This is a porthole?"

"Yes," FatherDam Chloe said. She stood and touched a button in the wall and the whole side of the room opened onto the blackness of *outside*.

Big, scary dark, eye-sizzling stars in different colors. Huge drifts of suns like roads to other places. And the green-blue planet dominating the view, getting bigger every minute.

All too big for Peaches, he moved close to FatherDam, let himself huddle by her feet since no one watched him.

"Wow," said the smooth-man-now-named-Apple. He stood and crossed to the window wall.

"From this view, it appears to be summer in the northern hemisphere," said the mate of red-headed woman. "I read the information you sent us on our new planet. That the angular tilt of Celta seems to be close to Earth's, even though the rotation is slower." His mouth quirked. "We'll be on Celta for some time before our new name month of Alder rolls around in the winter. Good. Gives me time to acclimate."

A slight silence fell, then FatherDam Chloe cackled, sounding in better humor. "Your wife is wrong in what she believes. She's reflecting old Earthan ideas of time. We, here on the Ship, are already *Celtans*. We celebrate the New Year on Samhain, November first. *Birch* is the first month of our year."

Captain Lady chuckled, then glanced at the woman's mate. "Sorry."

He just gave a tired smile and shrugged, but replied carefully. "I haven't studied our new religion that well, either, to know the attributes/characteristics of Alder."

The door opened and FamMan stepped in. "I was studying our new planet and informed that the porthole here, the best view, had been activated." He seemed easier, more confident. He'd been among people who respected him. Walking past Peaches, Randolph scrubbed his head in rough affection, then stood *right next to the window wall*! Peaches shivered.

"Magnificent view, isn't it?" Randolph asked.

"Something to tell our children and children's children," said smooth-man Apple.

A long breath came from the Alder, "Yes. I've yearned for space flight all of my life. I would have stayed awake the whole time, if it had been my decision."

"Best that you didn't," Captain Lady said softly. "Things did not go well." She stood on the far side of the room, angled so she could only see a little of the window. Peaches strolled to her and sat on her feet, giving them both comfort.

"No, things didn't go as we'd planned. It would have been a tragedy for my wife," now-Alder said.

FamMan Randolph cleared his throat. "The journey took very long, but we have developed a culture from the seeds you all planted. As for Alder," he dipped his head at the shorter man. "It is shield and defense, foundation."

"Good, good," the guy said.

"I can show you alder trees in the GreatGreensward if you like. Perhaps we've harvested wood. Very good for whistles and pipes, if you're musical."

A sweet smile graced the face of the Alder. "I'm not, but my daughter is. She and her husband came, too. They convinced us to buy into the project. They'll like the name, 'Alder.'"

"I'd like to see the GreatGreensward, too," Apple said. "In fact, I wanted to see that a whole lot more than come to this meeting."

Everyone else stood.

FatherDam Chloe said, "Randy, why don't you lead our friends on a tour of the GreatGreensward?"

She spoke to him like he hadn't become an adult the last month, more, like he hadn't reached his tenth Nameday.

With a brief nod to FatherDam Chloe, Randolph kept the doors open as everyone filed out, Captain Lady first, patting Randolph on the shoulder, then Apple and Alder the last of the colonists.

&.

Merry meet and merry part and may we merrily meet again.

CELTA HEARTMATE SERIES IN READING ORDER

Please note that these books and stories are primarily romances. They are not appropriate for children.
FOR BUYING LINKS, PLEASE SEE:
ALSO BY ROBIN D. OWENS

**Heart And Sword (story collection *Hearts and Swords;* this first story, Heart and Sword, takes place on board the generational starship Nuada's Sword)

Heart Fate

**Heart and Soul (story collection, Hearts and Swords)

Heart Change

ZANTH CLAIMS TREASURE (IN THIS BOOK)

Heart Journey

**Noble Heart (story collection, Hearts and Swords)

Heart Search

Heart Secret

Heart Fortune

Lost Heart (Novella)

Heart Fire

BACCAT CHOOSES HIS PERSON (IN THIS BOOK)

Heart Legacy

Heart Sight

ZANTH SAVES THE DAY (IN THIS BOOK)

HeartStones (a short story in Debris and Detritus)

ALSO BY ROBIN D. OWENS

Please note that these books and stories are primarily romances. They are not appropriate for children.

HeartMate

Heart Thief

Heart Duel

Heart Choice

Heart Quest

Heart Dance

Heart Fate

Heart Change

Heart Journey

Heart Search

Heart Secret

Heart Fortune

Lost Heart, a Celta Novella

Heart Fire

Heart Legacy

Heart Sight

Hearts And Swords, a Celta Story Collection

***

The Ghost Series (contemporary paranormal/ghost story romances)

Ghost Seer

Ghost Layer

Ghost Killer

Ghost Talker

Ghost Maker

* * *

Feral Magic, a contemporary paranormal shifter romance e-novella

Feral Magic

* * *

The Mystic Circle Series (contemporary fantasy)

Enchanted No More

Enchanted Again

Enchanted Ever After

* * *

The Summoning Series

Average American women are Summoned to another dimension to fight hideous evil, and, yes, with flying horses!

Guardian of Honor

Sorceress of Faith

Protector of the Flight

Keepers of the Flame

Echoes in the Dark

ABOUT THE AUTHOR

RITA® Award-winning author Robin D. Owens has been writing longer than she cares to recall. Her fantasy/futuristic romances found a home at Berkley with the issuance of HeartMate in December 2001. She credits the "telepathic cat with attitude" in selling that book. Currently, she has two domesticated cats (who have appeared in her stories).

She loves writing fantasy with romance or romance with fantasy, and particularly likes adding quirky characters for comic relief and leaving little threads dangling from book to book to see if readers pick up on them (usually, yes! Reader intelligence is awesome!).

Robin spends too much time on Facebook (see link below), loves hearing from readers, tries her best to respond to any questions and has been known to take reader advice for her work.When she receives good reviews or fan mail, she's been known to dance around bored cats...

Contact me here:

www.robindowens.com
robindowens@gmail.com

CELTA CATS COVER COPY

Smart Cats know what they want. And on the world of Celta, they are *very* smart . . . and magical. The cleverest cats can be Familiar Animal companions, bonded with a person.

Each of these six *never-before published* Celta Cat stories is told from the cat's point of view. They feature Peaches, the first Top Cat of Celta, two other Fams, and a trio of tales about that scrappy, favorite Fam, Zanth.

Peaches Arrives on Celta, Plenty of problems for Peaches to fix: challenges to his status; people spreading lies about Peaches' human companion and Peaches himself; Grandma's acting mean...and there's that very real concern that the Ship just might not land safely, fear he must overcome...

Zanth Gets His Boy, Zanth's meeting with a noble boy running from evil people changes both their lives in ways Zanth could never imagine

Pinky Becomes A Fam, Pinky is a smart enough cat to know that there is a difference in being a regular cat and a Familiar Companion Cat, and bonding better with his boy. He's determined to make the leap from cat to Fam, but doesn't realize exactly what that means...

Zanth Claims Treasure, Yes, the southern estate smells great, even better smelling is the glass orb full of magic that Zanth finds, and will fight to keep...

Baccat Chooses His Person, Life on the streets in the winter isn't what Baccat deserves, and he's determined to find a good person to take care of him. After all, he has so much to offer...but does he really deserve what he gets?

Zanth Saves The Day, A FamCat on a beach just can't sleep with all that irritating hatching and squeaking going on. Zanth finds new friends and defends them against bullies...